CHRONICLES ABROAD

Havana

CHRONICLES ABROAD

Havana

EDITED BY JOHN MILLER

AND SUSANNAH CLARK

CHRONICLE BOOKS
SAN FRANCISCO

Printed in Singapore.
Page 240 constitutes a continuation of the copyright page.

Library of Congress Cataloging-in-Publication Data available.
ISBN 0-8118-1058-5

Editing and design: Big Fish Books
Composition: Jennifer Petersen, Big Fish Books

Distributed in Canada by Raincoast Books,
8680 Cambie Street, Vancouver, B.C. V6P 6M9

10 9 8 7 6 5 4 3 2 1

Chronicle Books
275 Fifth Street
San Francisco, CA 94103

Contents

RICHARD HENRY DANA *Preface* ix

MARTHA GELLHORN *Cuba Revisited* 1

CRISTINA GARCIA *Dreaming in Cuban* 34

CONSUELO HERMER AND MARJORIE MAY *What to Wear* 56

FIDEL CASTRO *Cuban Childhood* 74

MARIO PUZO AND FRANCIS COPPOLA *The Godfather II* 98

SOPHIA PEABODY HAWTHORNE *The Cuba Journal, 1834* 114

GRAHAM GREENE *Our Man in Havana* 121

EDUARDO GALEANO *Chronicle of the City of Havana* 133

HENRY CABOT LODGE *The War with Spain* 136

ERNEST HEMINGWAY *Marlin off the Morro* 148

JAMES STEELE *Cuban Sketches* 161

MARGARITA ENGLE *Singing to Cuba* 172

MATURIN M. BALLOU *Creole Ladies, Marti the Smuggler, Bullfighting* 198

WALLACE STEVENS *Academic Discourse at Havana* 217

WILLIAM CULLEN BRYANT *Havana Letter* 223

ACKNOWLEDGMENTS 240

Richard Henry Dana

PREFACE

WE COAST THE northern shore of Cuba, from Matanzas westward. There is no waste of sand and low flats, as in most of our southern states; but the fertile, undulating land comes to the sea, and rises into high hills as it recedes. "There is the Morro! and right ahead!" "Why, there is the city too! Is the city on the sea? We thought it was on a harbor or bay." There, indeed, is the

After the overwhelming success of Two Years Before the Mast, *Richard Henry Dana (1815–1882) became a lawyer specializing in admiralty cases. Twenty-five years later, he traveled to Cuba and churned out* To Cuba and Back, *another best-seller, in two weeks.*

Morro, a stately hill of tawny rock, rising perpendicularly from the sea, and jutting into it, with walls and parapets and towers on its top, and flags and signals flying, and the tall lighthouse just in front of its outer wall. It is not very high, yet commands the sea about it. And there is the city, on the seacoast, indeed— the houses running down to the coral edge of the ocean. Where is the harbor, and where the shipping? Ah, there they are! We open an entrance, narrow and deep, between the beetling Morro and the Punta; and through the entrance, we see the spreading harbor and the innumerable masts. But the darkness is gathering, the sunset gun has been fired, we can just catch the dying notes of trumpets from the fortifications, and the Morro Lighthouse throws its gleam over the still sea. The little lights emerge and twinkle from the city. We are too late to enter the port, and slowly and reluctantly the ship turns her head off to seaward. The engine breathes heavily, and throws its one arm leisurely up and down; we rise and fall on the moonlit sea; the stars are near to us, or we are raised nearer to them; the Southern Cross is just above the horizon; and all night long, two streams of light lie upon the water, one of gold from the Morro, and one of silver from the moon. It is enchantment. Who can regret our delay, or wish to exchange this scene for the common, close anchorage of a harbor?

We are to go in at sunrise, and few, if any, are the passengers that are not on deck at the first glow of dawn. Before us lie the novel and exciting objects of the night before. The Steep Morro, with its tall sentinel lighthouse, and its towers and signal staffs and teeth of guns, is coming out into clear daylight; the red and yellow striped flag of Spain—blood and gold—floats over it. Point after point in the city becomes visible; the blue and white and yellow houses, with their roofs of dull red tiles, the quaint old Cathedral towers, and the almost endless lines of fortifications. The masts of the immense shipping rise over the headland, the signal for leave to enter is run up, and we steer in under full head, the morning gun thundering from the Morro, the trumpets braying and drums beating from all the fortifications, the Morro, the Punta, the long Cabaña, the Casa Blanca and the city walls, while the broad sun is fast rising over this magnificent spectacle.

Martha Gellhorn

CUBA REVISITED

THE FIRST MORNING in Havana, I stood by the sea-wall on the Malecon, feeling weepy with homesickness for this city. Like the exile returned; and ridiculous. I left Cuba forty-one years ago, never missed it and barely remembered it. A long amnesia, forgetting the light, the color of the sea and sky, the people, the charm of the place.

The Malecon is a nineteenth-century jewel and joke. Above their arcade, the mini-mansions rise three stories, each

---

Martha Gellhorn first visited Cuba with Ernest Hemingway in 1940, married him that year and left when they were divorced in 1946. Before finally returning in 1987, her career as a war correspondent took her to the Spanish Civil War, Normandy, Dachau on V-E day, and Vietnam.

house exuberantly different from the next: windows garlanded with plaster roses, Moorish pointy windows of stained glass, caryatids, ornate ironwork balconies, huge nail-studded carved doors. The paint on the stone buildings is faded to pastel, a ghostly reminder of former brilliance: pink trimmed with purple, blue with yellow, green with cobalt. Whoever lived here, when Cuba was my home from 1939 to May 1944, had departed: fluttering laundry suggested that their rich private houses were now multiple dwellings.

A delightful little black kid bounced out of somewhere, in spotless white shirt and royal blue shorts. He smiled up at me with a look of true love and undying trust. *"Rusa?"* he asked. I was mortally offended. Russian women of certain age, seen in Moscow, had bodies like tanks and legs like tree trunks.

"NO," I SAID crossly, *"Americana."* I should have said *"Norteamericana."* South of the U.S. border, people do not accept Americans' exclusive ownership of the continent.

The loving smile did not change. *"Da me chicle,"* he said. Give me chewing-gum. Cuba does not manufacture chewing-gum. In due course, I gathered that kids admire gum chewing as seen in American movies, still the most popular.

The Prado is a stylish old street with a wide central promenade: live oak trees, big light globes on wrought iron lamp-posts, benches. The benches were occupied by old women knitting and gossiping, old men reading papers and gossiping, poor people by our standards, looking comfortable and content. Now in the lunch-hour, groups of school children—from gleaming black to golden blonde—romped about the promenade, healthy, merry and as clean is if emerged from a washing-machine. The little ones wear a uniform of maroon shorts or mini-skirts, short-sleeved white shirts and a light blue neckerchief; the secondary school children wear canary yellow long pants or mini-skirts and a red neckerchief. The neckerchiefs show that they are Pioneers, blue for the babies, like Cubs and Scouts in my childhood.

Before, street boys would have drifted around here, selling lottery tickets or papers, collecting cigarette butts, offering to shine shoes, begging. They were funny and talkative, barefoot, dressed in dirty scraps, thin faces, thin bodies, nobody's concern. They did not attend school. Nor were they Afro-Cubans.

I had never thought of Cubans as blacks, and could only remember Juan, our pale mulatto chauffeur. Eventually I got that sorted out. A form of apartheid prevailed in central Havana, I don't know whether by edict or by landlords' decision not to rent to blacks. Presumably they could not get work either, unless as servants. But of course there were blacks in Cuba as everywhere else in the Caribbean, descendants of African slaves imported for the sugar-cane plantations. In my day, they must still have been concentrated in the eastern provinces, still cutting cane. Roughly one third of Cubans are of African or mixed blood, two thirds Caucasian.

Calle Obispo, formerly my beat for household supplies, had been turned into a pedestrian street. At one of the cross streets I saw the only cops I noticed in Havana, trying to disentangle a jam of trucks, motorcycles and hooting cars. The shops were a surprise: bikinis and cosmetics, fancy shoes, jewelry, a gift shop with china and glass ornaments. Not high fashion, but frivolous. And many bookstores, a real novelty; I remembered none. And a neighborhood store-front clinic.

Faces looked remarkably cheerful, unlike most city faces, and the street was enveloped in babble and laughter. Men met women, kissed them on the cheek, talked, moved on. That public friendly cheek-kissing astonished me; I had never seen it in a Latin American country, and never here in my day. Most of the women wore trousers made of a stretch material called, I think, crimplene; and most women were amply built. Their form-hugging pants were lavender, scarlet, emerald green, yellow, topped by blouses of flowered nylon. The young, boys and girls, wore jeans and T-shirts. T-shirts printed with Mickey Mouse, a big heart and LUV, UNIVERSITY OF MICHIGAN. Presents from relatives in the U.S.? Grown men wore proper trousers of lightweight gray or tan material and white shirts. These people were much better dressed than average Cubans before, and much better nourished.

At the top of this street, Salomon, a very small tubercular man of no definite age but great vitality, sold lottery tickets. Salomon was a communist and lived with the certainty of a glorious communist future, when everyone would eat a lot and earn their keep by useful work. I remembered him out of nowhere, and hoped with all my heart that he lived to see his dream come true, but doubted it; Salomon didn't look then as if he had the necessary fifteen years left.

I was staying at the Hotel Deauville, a post-war, pre-Revolución blight on the Malecon. It is a plum-colored cement Bauhaus-style tower. I came to dote on the hideous Deauville because of the staff, jokey and friendly with each other and the guests. The Deauville is classed as three-star, not suitable for rich dollar tourists. My room with bath cost $26. Like all tourist hotels, the Deauville has its own Duty-Free Shop. Tourists of every nationality pay for everything in U.S. dollars. You are given your change, down to nickels and dimes, in American money. For practical purposes one dollar equals one Cuban peso, a parallel economy for natives and tourists. President Reagan has tightened the permanent U.S. economic embargo to include people. Cuba is off limits to American tourists. But that year, 1985, 200,000 capitalist tourists, from Canada, Europe, Mexico, South America, uninterested in or undaunted by communism, had caught on to the idea of the cheapest Caribbean holiday.

At the Deauville, I had my first view of the amusing and economical national mini-skirt: above-the-knee uniform for women employees, different colors for different occupations. And was also plunged into the national custom of calling everyone by first names, beginning with Fidel who is called nothing else. I was rather testy, to start, hearing "Marta" from one and all and the intimate *tu* instead of *usted,* a disappearing formality. But I quickly adjusted and was soon addressing strangers as *compañero* or *compañera.* You cannot say comrad (American) or comraid (British) without feeling silly, but *compañero* has the cozy sound of a companion.

I WANTED TO be on my way. I had not come to Cuba to study communism but to snorkel. At the Cuban Embassy in London, I found some tourist bumf, describing a new glamorous hotel at Puerto Escondido, which included the magic word, snorkeling. I was going to Nicaragua, serious business, and meant to treat myself *en route* to two weeks mainly in the lovely turquoise shallows off the Cuban coast. A couple of days in Havana, to retrace my distant past; then sun, snorkeling, thrillers, rum drinks: my winter holiday.

You can go anywhere you want in Cuba, except to the American naval base at Guantanamo on the eastern tip of the island—an extraordinary piece of property which most foreigners do not know is held and operated by the United States. You can hire, with or without driver, a small Russian Lada sedan belonging to INTUR, the Ministry of Tourism. The Lada is as tough as a Land Rover, Third World model, with iron-hard upholstery and, judging by sensation, no springs. I asked INTUR for a car with driver, intending to look over the hotel at Puerto Escondido, the goal of my Cuban trip.

The driver, rightly named Amable, said that Puerto Escondido was half an hour from Havana; my introduction to Cuban optimism. "No problem" might be the national motto; it is the one English phrase everyone can say. We drove through the tunnel under Havana harbor, new to me, and along the superhighway, adorned with billboards, very depressing: progress. The billboards are exhortations, not advertisements. A light bulb, with ENERGÍA in huge letters and a plea to save it. A bag of coins and a single-stroke dollar sign for the peso, recommending the public to bank their money at two-and-a-half percent interest. Many patriotic billboards: "WE WOULD DIE BEFORE WE GIVE UP OUR PRINCIPLES." Two hours from Havana found us bumping on a mud road through lush jungle scenery. A solitary soldier stopped us where the track ended. Puerto Escondido was not finished; it would be ready next year. More Cuban optimism. The soldier suggested a tourist resort at Jibacoa further on.

Amable managed to find Jibacoa—small brick houses, newly landscaped—and a bar and a restaurant. At the bar two Canadian girls, secretaries from Toronto who had arrived yesterday, were full of enthusiasm and information. They had a nice double room; the food was "interesting"; rape was punished by shooting; Cubans were lovely people; and they looked forward to a night out at the Tropicana, Havana's answer to the Paris Lido. Goody, but what about snorkeling? A man in a wet-suit was coming up from the beach; the girls said he was Luis, in charge of water sports. Luis guaranteed that the snorkeling was fine and we both stared to the north where clouds like solid black smoke spread over the sky.

"*Un norte?*" I asked with dismay. I remembered only perfect winter weather.

"Yes, come back in a few days when it is past."

But it did not pass.

By morning, the sea was greenish black, matching the black sky. Waves smashed across the Malecon, closed to traffic, and drove sand and pebbles up the side streets. The wind was at gale force; it rained. A gigantic storm and worsening. I was cold and slumped into travel despair, an acute form of boredom. With no enthusiasm, I arranged to fill time, meeting people and seeing sights, until the storm ended.

THE DISTINGUISHED Afro-Cuban poet and I talked in the crowded lobby of the Hotel Nacional, an old four-star hotel. Suddenly she made a sound of disgust and said, "I hate that stupid out-of-date stuff." She spoke perfect American. The object of her disgust was a wedding party: bride in white with veil, groom in tuxedo, flower girls, bridesmaids, beaming parents and guests, headed for the wedding reception. I was pleased that the out-of-date could be freely practiced by those who wanted it.

I had an important question to ask her but was very unsure of my ground. "Something puzzles me," I said. "Fidel made a decree or whatever, as soon as the Revolución started, forbidding racism. I mean, he said it was over; there wouldn't be any more. And there isn't. Surely that is amazing?" It sure is. Even more amazing, it seems to work.

"Of course you can't change people's prejudices by law; you can't change what they feel in their hearts. But you can make any racist acts illegal and punish them. We hope that as we live together more and know each other better as human beings, the prejudices will disappear."

We had no racist problem she and I, just the wrong vibes. She thought me too light; I thought her too heavy.

I was interested in how writers earned their livings. Very few of the 600 members of the Writers' Union can live by books alone, like us. There are many publishing houses, state-owned but managed by distinct staffs for a varied public. You submit your manuscript; if accepted, you get sixty percent of the retail price of the first edition, whether the books are sold or not; then forty percent of further editions. Cubans love poetry, so poets abound and are widely read.

FEELING DULL BUT dutiful, I went to look at Alamar—a big housing estate, white rectangular factories for living spread over the green land off the highway outside of Havana.

"Marta, why do you say you do not like such a place? I have friends there. They have a very nice apartment." Today's driver, called Achun, part Chinese, had served in Angola. He said he was truly sorry for those Africans; they were a hundred years behind Cuba.

I asked, "How big?"

"Two bedrooms, three, four, depending on the number of the family."

I told him about vandalism as we know it. Achun was dumbfounded.

"Why would people ruin their own homes?"

Close-up, Alamar was not bad; no graffiti on the white walls, no broken windows—on the contrary, shined and curtained—a skimpy fringe of flowers around each building, and thin new trees. The buildings are four stories high, widely separated by lawn.

"The cinema is behind those buildings," Achun said.

Here the bus stopped; a few weary people were piling out. The forty-minute ride to and from Havana in the always overcrowded buses has to be a trial. (Havana is about to get a needed metro system.) This central shopping area reduced me to instant gloom. I thought at first it was filthy. The impression of grime was not due to dirt but to unpainted cement. Of course Cuba is poor and needs many things more vital than paint, yet it distressed me that these people, who adore bright color, must be denied it.

The bookstore was attractive because of the gaudy book covers. A soldier and a child were the only customers in the middle of a chilly grey weekday afternoon. A corner of the room had been set aside for children's books. The paper is coarse, the covers thin, but books cost from forty-five to seventy-five cents.

"Each year we have a quota," said the middle-aged saleslady. "And every year we exceed it."

"How can you have a quota? You can't force people to buy books, can you?"

"Oh no, it is not like that. Every year we are sent a quota of books and every year we must ask for more, because they are sold. All ages buy books. Fidel said, 'Everything basic to the people must be cheap. Books are basics.' "

"What is most popular?"

"Detectives and romantic novels."

I DROVE AROUND Havana, sightseeing, half-curious, and wholly sick of the miserable weather. I chatted in the dingy main market where the toy counter and meat and poultry counter were the busiest. I asked about fares at the jammed railroad station, learning that the best fast train to the other end of the island costs $10.50. I cruised through the stylish section of Vedado with the big hotels, airline offices, shops, restaurants, movies and the large Edwardian houses. I peered at the Miramar mansions. The rich departed Cubans left a bountiful gift to the Revolución, all their grand homes and classy apartment buildings. The big houses are clinics, kindergartens, clubs for trade unions, and whatever has no public use is portioned off for private living space.

Then I decided I needed some action and barged into a secondary school, announcing that I was a foreign journalist and would like to sit in on a class and see how they taught their students. This caused extreme confusion. (As it probably would if I barged into the Chepstow comprehensive.) The school sent me to the local Poder Popular office where I met the very cornerstone of bureaucracy: the woman at the door. Behind a desk/table/counter in every government office is a woman, preferably middle-aged; her job is to keep people out. Poder Popular sent me to the Ministry of Education. There the woman at the door said that Public Relations at INTUR, the Ministry of Tourism, must write to Public Relations at the Ministry of Education. I reported this to INTUR, decrying it as an absurd fuss about nothing. INTUR promised that a school visit would be arranged. "Be patient, Marta," said Rosa, an INTUR director. "Everything is done through organizations here."

To their credit, the Ministry of Education sent me to a very modest school in a poor suburb. The Secondary School of the Martyrs of Guanabacoa. The driver could not find it. We were twenty minutes late. I got out of the Lada and saw school kids in canary yellow lined up along the path to the front door and a greeting committee of adults. I apologized unhappily for keeping everyone waiting and walked past the honor guard, feeling absurd. Instead of a twenty-one-gun salute, I got a shouted slogan. On the school steps a little Afro-Cuban girl stepped from the ranks, shouted something and behind her the official chorus shouted an answer. This went on for several minutes but I could not decipher a single shouted word. I was then presented with a sheaf of gladioli and lilies in cellophane and began to feel as if I were the Queen Mother.

The man in charge, whose position I never understood, presented the school principal, a large shy Afro-Cuban woman in dark blue crimplene trousers and white blouse. I was shown the school bulletin board with its smiling photographs of the "martyrs"—handsome girls and boys, not much older than the children here, killed by

Batista's police for their clandestine work in the Revolución. Asked what I would like to visit, I said the English class. The school was unpainted cement inside and out, built on the cheap in 1979.

The English teacher was nervous and nice and desperately eager for his class to perform well. Each child read aloud a sentence from their textbook, dealing with Millie's birthday party. Offhand, I could not think of a deadlier subject. *"Toothbrush and toothpaste."* [Millie's birthday presents!] "are very hard for them to say; also *room.*" His own accent was odd; the kids were choked with stage fright, rivaling mine.

A bell blessedly rang. Here, the children stay in one room, the teachers move. It was the history hour in another classroom. The children—the top form, aged fifteen—rose to their feet and shouted a slogan, led by the elected class prefect who was always a girl. Hard to understand, but it sounded like promising Fidel to study and be worthy of the Revolución. Each class devised its own slogan, a new one every month, and five times a day, at the start of their class periods, they shouted this at the teacher. The history teacher was a thin intense shabbily-dressed young man who described the sugar crises of 1921, when prices fell and the people suffered despair and starvation though their work had enriched the bourgeoisie and the American capitalists. I wanted to say that American workers suffered too in times of depression and unemployment, but didn't feel that speech-making was part of my new role.

Biology was taught by a stout *mulata compañera* in lavender pants, and taught brilliantly. The subject for the day was the renal system, up to that moment a total mystery to me. All the kids raised their hands, competing to answer. This subject—their bodies—clearly interested them much more than history or English. After class, the teacher explained that by the end of the term they would have studied the sexual organs, the nine months of pregnancy and birth. To finish, they would discuss "the human couple, and the need for them to be equals and share the same ideals and interests." She showed me their laboratory, a small room with a few Bunsen burners. Her only teaching-aid was a plaster human torso, open at the front, with all the brightly-colored alarming organs in place.

There were 579 children, more Caucasian than Afro-Cuban, and fifty teachers, about equally divided as to color and sex. School is compulsory through the ninth grade, age fifteen. After that, children can choose to continue for three years in pre-university studies or technical schools, according to their grades. At eighteen, the boys do military service, but university students are exempt since Cuba needs all the professionals it can train.

Snacks had been laid out in the principal's office. I looked at these poorly-dressed men and women and grieved to think of them chipping in for this party. They were so excited about me because the school had never received a visitor before, no Cuban personage, let alone a foreigner. They spoke of their students with pride; it must feel good to teach such lively and willing children. Never mind that they had no library, no workshop, no gym, no proper laboratory in this bleak building. The staff invented substitutes and got on with the job. I asked to meet the Head Prefect, elected by her peers. She was a lovely tall slim girl, almost inaudible from shyness, blonde with green eyes. She said that the entire school went on two camping weekends a year and for a week to Varadero, Cuba's famous beach. The top student (this girl) joined all the other secondary school top-graders for a whole summer month at Varadero. Fun and sport as a reward for work. I remember winning a school prize, a richly-bound uninteresting book.

I liked everyone and told them they had a fine school, meaning it, and thanked them for the visit. In the Lada, returning to Havana, I gave my character a shake and became again a normal, not a Very Important, person.

As I was about to leave Cuba, the sky cleared. On a sunny morning I collected Gregorio and we went to visit my former home, the Finca Vigía, fifteen miles outside Havana, now a museum or indeed a shrine. Gregorio is eighty-seven years old, the only link to my Cuban past and the only Cuban repository of Hemingway lore, as he was the sailor-guardian of Hemingway's boat, the *Pilar*, for twenty-three years. People come from far and wide to hear his verbatim memories, which he quotes like Scripture. Hemingway and he were the same age. His devotion to his patron-hero is genuine and time has added luster to that devotion. The *Pilar* years were surely the best for Gregorio. He is a tall thin weather-beaten man, with calm natural dignity. He was liked and respected—thought, typically, to have the finest qualities of a Spaniard. Not that anybody troubled about his separate existence; I had never seen his house.

The Museo Hemingway, temporarily closed to the public for repairs, is wildly popular with Cubans. They come again and again, bringing picnics to spend the day, after a respectful tour of the house. The long driveway is flanked by towering royal palms and sumptuous jacaranda trees. I couldn't believe my eyes; I remembered nothing so imposing. The driveway curved to show the house, now glaring white and naked. "It looks like a sanatorium," I said. "What did they do to the ceiba?"

Forty-six years ago, I found this house through an advertisement and rented it, for one hundred dollars a month, indifferent to its sloppiness, because of the giant ceiba growing from the wide front steps. Any house with such a tree was perfect in my eyes. Besides, the terrace beyond the steps was covered by a trellis roof of brilliant bougainvillaea. Flowering vines climbed up the wall behind the ceiba; orchids grew from its trunk. All around the house were acres of high grass, hiding caches of empty gin bottles, and rusty tins, and trees. The house was almost invisible, but painted an unappetizing yellow; I had it painted a dusty pale pink; the Museo changed it to glaring white. The great tree was always the glory of the finca.

"The roots were pulling up the floor of the house. The Museo had to cut it down," Gregorio said.

"They should have pulled down the house instead."

I never saw a ceiba like it, anywhere. The enormous trunk, the color and texture of elephant hide, usually dwarfs the branches of the ceiba. But this one had branches thick as other tree trunks, spreading in wide graceful loops; it was probably several hundred years old. The house is a pleasant old one-story affair of no special style; the six rooms are large and well proportioned, full of light.

The members of the museum staff have their office in the former garage; they are earnest, devout keepers of the shrine. I recognized all the furniture I had ordered from the local carpenter, and lapsed into giggles over the later addition of stuffed animal heads and horns on every wall. In the master's bedroom, the biggest buffalo head I had ever seen, including hundreds on the hoof, glowered over the desk. True, I had never been so close to any buffalo, living or dead. "He did not write here," said one of the staff. He wrote *For Whom the Bell Tolls* at this desk, but that was pre-buffalo.

The house depressed me; I hurried through it, eager to get back to the trees. How had I taken for granted this richness? Then it struck me: time, the years of my life at last made real. The trees had been growing in splendor for forty-one years— the immense mangoes and flamboyantes and palms and jacarandas and avocates were all here before, but young then like me.

I had definitely forgotten the size and the elegant shape of the swimming-pool. Gregorio was interested in two large cement cradles, placed where the tennis court used to be. The *Pilar* was his inheritance, he had cared for it and given it to the state, and it was to be brought here and placed on these cradles.

"Like the *Granma*," I said, and everyone looked slightly shocked at the irreverence. The *Granma* is the large cabin cruiser that bore Fidel and his followers from Mexico to Cuba in 1956: the transport of the Revolución. It is enshrined in a glass case in a small park in Old Havana. As an object of patriotic veneration, a lot jollier than Lenin embalmed. It seems that *Granma*, now the name of a province and of the major national newspaper, is simply a misspelling of Grandma, which is delightful.

The visit was as fast as I could make it—handshakes, compliments standing under a beautiful jacaranda by the garage—and we were off to Gregorio's house in the fishing village of Cojimar. The visit to the Museo had been a duty call; it was expected. I wanted to listen to Gregorio.

In the car, I began to have faintly turbulent emotions. I remembered with what gaiety I had come to this country and how I had left, frozen in distaste of a life that seemed to me hollow and boring to die. Looking after the finca ate my time, but was worth it because of the beauty. Then Cuba became worth nothing, a waste of time. Cuba now is immeasurably better than the mindless feudal Cuba I knew. But no place for a self-willed, opinionated loner, which is what I suppose I am. Never a team-player—though I wish this team, this people, well, and hope it improves, as it has, year by year.

"Gregorio, it is a comfort that nobody is hungry."

Gregorio looked at me and smiled. "You remember that?"

"Yes."

"*Pues sí,* Marta, nobody is hungry now."

Gregorio has owned his small cement house since 1936 and it is freshly painted, sky blue and white. Gregorio was still anxious about his wife, *mi señora* he calls her in the old way, who fell off a ladder weeks ago and broke her thigh. She was waiting for us indoors, in a chair, her leg in plaster. She kissed me, told me I was "very well preserved," and they both recounted the saga of the leg. They have a telephone; the ambulance came at once; she was taken to the hospital and operated on. " 'A big operation,' the doctor said." Gregorio's turn: "Very big. He said at our age the bones are like glass." She stayed twenty days in the hospital, then the ambulance brought her home. The doctor from the local polyclinic came every day to check her condition, now he only comes once a week. "Not a cent, Marta, you understand. It did not cost even one centavo."

Gregorio has a monthly pension of 170 pesos (call it pre-inflation dollars); actually a large pension, due to his long work years. Still, I thought this a skimpy sum until they told me the price system: six dollars a month flat for the telephone, which is a luxury; three dollars flat for electricity—and they have an electric fridge and cooker and water heater; the color TV is bought on the never-never, at ten percent a month of salary or pension. The food ration is extremely cheap.

"Is there enough food?"

"Yes, yes, more than enough, but if you want different things you buy them. It costs more." Clothes are also rationed and cheap; they would not need or want more than the yearly quota of shoes, shirts, underclothes etc. "Young people care for clothes, they buy more off rations. And education is free too, Marta."

His middle-aged daughter now arrived; she is volubly enthusiastic about the new Cuba. Then his granddaughter appeared with a pink and white baby in her arms, Gregorio's great grandson, on her way to his weekly checkup at the polyclinic. Each generation owns its little house in this village.

I felt that Gregorio was getting a trifle restive among all these females so we moved to the front porch to smoke. He brought out a bottle of Cuban rum. "As long as I have this," he said, pouring me a hefty slug, "and my cigars, I am content." Now talking soberly he said, "Marta, all the intelligentsia left, all of them." I was baffled by the word: what would Gregorio know of intelligentsia? Then I guessed he meant the world he had known with Hemingway, the Sunday parties with the jai-alai players at the finca, parties at the Cojimar pub, the carefree company of the rich and privileged, the big-game fishermen, the members of the pigeon-shooting club, and though I had never seen the Country Club he meant that circle too, since the *Pilar* was berthed there in later years. He may have missed the glamour of a life he shared and did not share. But he had met Fidel. "I think he is a good man," Gregorio said. After Hemingway left in 1959, Gregorio returned to his old profession of fisherman, then retired and became unofficial adviser to the Museo Hemingway. "I have never had any trouble with anyone."

I asked about the few Cubans I could remember by name; they had all long decamped. I asked about the Basque jai-alai players, exiles from Franco's Spain, who had fought for their homeland and lost. I loved them, brave and high-spirited men who never spoke of the past, not expecting to see their country and families again.

"They left when Batista took power. They did not like dictatorship. There was much killing with Batista, in secret. I heard that Patchi died."

"Patchi!" I was stunned. "And Ermua?" Ermua was the great *pelotari* who moved like a panther and was the funniest, the wildest of them all.

"Yes, he died too."

"How could he? Why? So young?"

And suddenly I realized that Patchi was probably my age, Ermua maybe five years younger; they need not have died young.

"Gregorio, I am growing sad. Cuba makes me understand that I am old."

"I too." Gregorio laughed. "*Pues, no hay remedio.*"

MY BAG WAS packed, my bill paid and I had nothing to do until two A.M. when I took the plane to Nicaragua. I went back to Jibacoa where I had gone in hope of snorkeling on my first day. Now the weather was the way it ought to be, brilliantly blue cloudless sky, hot sun. I went to the Cuban resort, not the foreigners' tourist domain on the hill. There were dozens of small cabins for two or four people, a boat-yard with rentable pleasure craft, an indoor recreation room, ping-pong and billiards, a snack bar to provide the usual foul American white bread sandwiches and a restaurant. The main feature was a beautiful long white sand beach, bracketed by stony headlands. Where there are rocks there are fish. I was loaned a cabin to change in and a towel: no, no, you pay nothing, you are not sleeping here. I could never decide whether I was treated with unfailing kindness because I was a foreigner or because of my age.

There were many people on the beach, looking happy in the lovely weather, all ages, sunbathing, swimming, picnicking. A young man offered me his deck-chair so that I could read and bake comfortably between swims. I put on my mask and plunged in, feeling the water cold after the storm, but bursting with joy to see familiar fish, special favorites being a shoal of pale blue ovoid fish with large smiles marked in black on their faces. In my old Cuban days, I wore motorcyclist's goggles; masks and snorkels had not been invented.

When I returned to my deck-chair at the far end of the beach, I found two small fat white bodies lying face down near me. After a while they worried me, and I warned them in Spanish that they were getting a dangerous burn. A grey-haired man sat up and said, "Spik Engleesh?" They were "Greek-Canadians" from the tourist resort above; they liked the place, they even liked the food. He said, "They work slow. No, lady, I don't think it's the climate. But they're happy. The guy who looks after our group is doing double time. For that, he gets a month off." He smiled, he shrugged.

From nine to five, the tour guide would be on hand to interpret if needed, to coddle the old if they wanted it, swim with the girls, play table tennis, eat, drink. Maybe he would take them on a day sight-seeing tour of Havana. And then, from five to one in the morning, if anyone was still awake, he would do the same, except he would drink more than swim, and dance with the girls to radio music in the bar, and of course escort them all on the big night out at the Tropicana. The Greek-Canadian's shrug and smile said clearly that he did not consider this to be hardship duty. Here was a small-scale capitalist deriding the easy life of the communists. Soft communism, a comic turn-around from the dreaded American accusation: "soft on communism." I thought it the best joke yet.

Cristina Garcia

DREAMING IN CUBAN

THE LATE AFTERNOON downpour sends the students'
mothers scurrying under the coral tree in the yard of the Niko-
lai Lenin Elementary School. A lizard vibrates in the crook of
the tree's thickest branch. Celia stands alone in the rain in her
leather pumps and jade housedress waiting for her twin granddaughters to return from their camping trip to the Isle of
Pines. It seems to her that she has spent her entire life waiting
for others, for something or other to happen. Waiting for her
lover to return from Spain. Waiting for the summer rains to

*Cristina Garcia was born in Havana in 1958 and grew up in New York
City. She later worked as a correspondent for* Time *in Miami, San Francisco,
and Los Angeles, where she lives today.* Dreaming in Cuban *is her first novel.*

end. Waiting for her husband to leave on his business trips so she could play Debussy on the piano.

The waiting began in 1934, the spring before she married Jorge del Pino, when she was still Celia Almeida. She was selling American photographic equipment at El Encanto, Havana's most prestigious department store, when Gustavo Sierra de Armas strode up to her display case and asked to see Kodak's smallest camera. He was a married Spanish lawyer from Granada and said that he wanted to document the murders in Spain through a peephole in his overcoat. When the war came, no one could refute his evidence.

Gustavo returned to Celia's counter again and again. He brought her butterfly jasmine, the symbol of patriotism and purity, and told her that Cuba, too, would one day be free of blood-suckers. Gustavo sang to her beauty mark, the *lunar* by her mouth. He bought her drop pearl earrings.

Ese lunar que tienes, cielito lindo,
junto a la boca . . .

No se lo des a nadie, cielito lindo,
que a mí me toca.

When Gustavo left her to return to Spain, Celia was inconsolable. The spring rains made her edgy, the greenery hurt her eyes. She saw mourning doves peck at carrion on her doorstep and visited the *botánicas* for untried potions.

"I want a long, easy solace," she told the *gitanas.*

She bought tiger root from Jamaica to scrape, a cluster of indigo, translucent crimson seeds, and lastly, a tiny burlap pouch of herbs. She boiled teas and honeycombs, steamed open her pores, adjusted the shutters, and drank.

Celia took to her bed by early summer and stayed there for the next eight months. That she was shrinking there was no doubt. Celia had been a tall woman, a head taller than most men, with a full bosom and slender, muscled legs. Soon she was a fragile pile of opaque bones, with yellowed nails and no monthly blood. Her great-aunt Alicia wrapped Celia's thinning hair with colorful bandannas, making her appearance all the more startling.

The doctors could find nothing wrong with Celia. They examined her through monocles and magnifying glasses, with metal instruments that embossed her chest and forearms, thighs and forehead with a blue geometry. With pencil-thin flashlights they peered into her eyes, which hung like lanterns in her sleepless face. They prescribed vitamins and sugar pills and pills to make her sleep, but Celia diminished, ever more pallid, in her bed.

Neighbors suggested their own remedies: arnica compresses, packed mud from a holy well, ground elephant tusk from the Niger to mix in her daily broth. They dug up the front yard for buried maledictions but found nothing. The best cooks on Palmas Street offered Celia coconut custard, *guayaba* and cheese tortes, bread pudding, and pineapple cakes. Vilma Castillo lit a baked Alaska that set the kitchen aflame and required many buckets of water to extinguish. After the fire, few people came to visit Celia. "She is determined to die," they concluded.

Desperate, her great-aunt called a *santera* from Regla, who draped Celia with beaded necklaces and tossed shells to divine the will of the gods.

"Miss Celia, I see a wet landscape in your palm," the little *santera* said, then turned to Tía Alicia. "She will survive the hard flames."

CELIA WROTE HER first letter to Gustavo Sierra de Armas upon the insistence of Jorge del Pino, who came courting during her housebound exile. Jorge was fourteen years older than she and wore round steel glasses that shrank his blue eyes. Celia had known him since she was a child, when her mother had sent her from the countryside to live with her great-aunt in Havana.

"Write to that fool," Jorge insisted. "If he doesn't answer, you will marry me."

November 11, 1934
Mi querido Gustavo,
　　A fish swims in my lung. Without you,
what is there to celebrate?
I am yours always,
　　　　Celia

FOR TWENTY-FIVE years, Celia wrote her Spanish lover a letter on the eleventh day of each month, then stored it in a satin-covered chest beneath her bed. Celia has removed her drop pearl earrings only nine times, to clean them. No one ever remembers her without them.

CELIA'S TWIN GRANDDAUGHTERS recount how on their camping trip they fed midget bananas to a speckled horse and examined horned earthworms peculiar to the island. Celia knows that Luz and Milagro are always alone with one another, speaking in symbols only they understand. Luz, older by twelve minutes, usually speaks for the two of them. The sisters are double stones of a single fruit, darker than their mother, with rounder features and their father's inky eyes. They have identical birthmarks, diminutive caramel crescents over their left eyelids, and their braids hang in duplicate ropes down their backs.

The three of them hitch a ride to the house on Palmas Street. Their driver, a balding man with gently serrated teeth, shakes Celia's hand with fingers the texture of cork. She correctly surmises that he is a plumber. Celia has prided herself on guessing occupations since her days at El Encanto, when she could precisely gauge how much a customer had to spend on a camera. Her biggest sales went to Americans from Pennsylvania. What did they take so many pictures of up there?

The driver turns left on Palmas Street with its matched rows of closely set two-story houses, all painted a flamboyant yellow. Last fall, the line at the hardware store snaked around the block for the surplus paint, left over from a hospital project on the other side of Havana. Felicia bought the maximum amount allowed, eight gallons, and spent two Sundays painting the house with borrowed brushes and ladders.

"After all," she said, "you could die waiting for the right shade of blue."

The air is damp from the afternoon rains. Celia gathers her granddaughters close. "Your grandfather died last week," she tells them, then kisses each one on the cheek. She takes Luz and Milagro by the hand and walks up the front steps of the house on Palmas Street.

"My girls! My girls!" Felicia waves at them frantically from the second-story bedroom window, lost behind the tamarind tree heavy with sparrows and tawny pods. Her face is spotted and enlivened with heat. She is wearing her American-made flannel nightgown with the pale blue roses. It is buttoned to the top of her throat. "I made coconut ice cream!"

Store-bought ice cream is cheap, but for Felicia, making ice cream from scratch is part of the ritual that began after her husband left in 1966. Felicia's delusions commence suddenly, frequently after heavy rains. She rarely deviates from her original pattern, her hymn of particulars.

Felicia coaxes her young son to join her. Celia and her granddaughters enter the house on Palmas Street, to find Ivanito, his dimpled hands clasped, singing the lyrics to a melodramatic love song.

> *Quieres regresar, pero es imposible*
> *Ya mi corazón se encuentra rebelde*
> *Vuélvete otra vez*
> *Que no te amaré jamás*

THAT NIGHT, CELIA lies awake in the bare dining room of the yellow house on Palmas Street, the house that once belonged to her mother-in-law and where Felicia now lives. Sleep is an impossibility in this room, in this bed with memories that plague her for days. This house, Celia thinks, has brought only misfortune.

She remembers when she returned from her honeymoon in Soroa with a white orchid in her hair, one that Jorge had clipped from the terraced gardens high above the sulfur baths. Her mother-in-law, who had a fleshy-tipped nose and a pendulous, manly face, snatched the flower from Celia's ear and crushed it in her hand.

"I will have no harlotry in my house," Berta Arango del Pino snapped, staring hard at the darkened mole by Celia's mouth.

Then she turned to her only son.

"I'll fry you a red snapper, *mi corazón*, just the way you like it."

JORGE'S BUSINESS TRIPS stretched unendurably. During the first months of their marriage, he called Celia every night, his gentle voice assuaging her. But soon his calls came less frequently, and his voice lost its comforting tone.

When he was home, they made love tensely and soundlessly while his mother slept. Their marriage bed was a narrow cot that was hidden in the dining-room closet during the day. Afterward, they would dress themselves in their night-clothes and fall asleep in each other's arms. At dawn, Berta Arango del Pino would enter with a short knock, open the shutters, and announce breakfast.

Celia wanted to tell Jorge how his mother and his sister, Ofelia, scorned her, how they ate together in the evenings without inviting her. "Did you see the shirt she sewed for our Jorge today?" she heard Ofelia scoff. "She must think he's growing a third arm." They left her scraps to eat, worse than what they fed the dogs in the street.

One day, while the two of them went to buy embroidery threads, Celia decided to cook them a savory flank-steak stew. She set the dining-room table with the good linen and silverware, collected fruit from the tamarind tree, and squeezed and strained a pitcherful of juice. Hopeful and nervous, she waited for their return. Ofelia got to the kitchen first.

"What do you think you're doing?" she said, opening and closing the lid of the pot like a cymbal.

Berta Arango del Pino followed on her thick-ankled legs. She took two dishrags and carried the pot impassively through the living room, down the front steps and across the yard, then poured the steaming casserole into the gutter.

JORGE'S MOTHER AND his sister played dominoes in the dining room until late, delaying Celia's sleep, her only solace. Celia knew that Ofelia joined her mother at her dressing table, where they sat on their bony behinds and rubbed whitening cream into their dark, freckled faces. Berta Arango del Pino left the paste on overnight to remove any evidence of her mulatto blood. She had a taste for absinthe, too, and exuded a faint licorice smell. In the mornings, her cheeks and forehead burned from the bleach and the potent liqueur.

On Saturdays, she and Ofelia went to the beauty parlor and returned with identical helmets of girlish curls, which they protected fiercely with hairpins and kerchiefs. Ofelia still hoped for suitors although her mother had long since driven off the few men that dared come around, nervously clutching flowers or mints. She wore her decorous dresses to morning mass, and around her neck displayed the short single strand of pearls she had received on her fifteenth birthday.

Ofelia was afraid of the attention men once paid her but seemed more fearful now of her invisibility. In quiet moments she must have asked: Who am I whitening my skin for? Who notices the tortoiseshell combs in my hair? Would anyone care if the seams on my stockings were crooked? Or if I didn't wear any at all?

CELIA AWOKE ONE morning and knew she was pregnant. She felt as if she had swallowed a bell. The rigid edges of her wedding ring sliced into her tumid finger. Days passed but her husband did not call. She took Ofelia aside and told her in confidence, but Ofelia absently touched her own milkless breasts and ran with the news to her mother.

"The indecency!" Berta Arango del Pino protested. "How many more mouths can my poor son feed?"

Ofelia took to appropriating Celia's dresses and shoes. "You won't be needing this anymore," she said, clutching a cream linen suit, which hung better on the wire hanger than on her desiccated frame. "After the baby, none of this will fit you anyway." She stole Celia's leather pumps when her feet got too swollen to wear them and tore the backs open with her calcarated heels.

Celia wished for a boy, a son who could make his way in the world. If she had a son, she would leave Jorge and sail to Spain, to Granada. She would dance flamenco, her skirts whipping a thousand crimson lights. Her hands would be hummingbirds of hard black sounds, her feet supple against the floorboards of the night. She would drink whiskey with tourists, embroider histories flagrant with peril, stride through the darkness with nothing but a tambourine and too many carnations. One night, Gustavo Sierra de Armas would enter her club, walk onstage, and kiss her deeply to violent guitars.

If she had a girl, Celia decided, she would stay. She would not abandon a daughter to this life, but train her to read the columns of blood and numbers in men's eyes, to understand the morphology of survival. Her daughter, too, would outlast the hard flames.

Jorge named their daughter Lourdes for the miracle-working shrine of France. In the final dialogue with her husband, before he took her to the asylum, Celia talked about how the baby had no shadow, how the earth in its hunger had consumed it. She held their child by one leg, handed her to Jorge, and said, "I will not remember her name."

AFTER HER SLEEPLESS night in the house on Palmas Street, Celia wanders to the ceiba tree in the corner of the Plaza de las Armas. Fruit and coins are strewn by its trunk and the ground around the tree bulges with buried offerings. Celia knows that good charms and bad are hidden in the stirred earth near its sacred roots. Tía Alicia told her once that the ceiba is a saint, female and maternal. She asks the tree permission before crossing its shadow, then circles it three times and makes a wish for Felicia.

Celia rests in the interior patio of the plaza, where royal palms dwarf a marble statue of Christopher Columbus. Inside the museum there's a bronze weathervane of Doña Inés de Bobadilla, Cuba's first woman governor, holding the Cross of Calatrava. She became governor of the island after her husband, Hernando de Soto, left to conquer Florida. Doña Inés, it is said, was frequently seen staring out to sea, searching the horizon for her husband. But de Soto died on the banks of the Mississippi River without ever seeing his wife again.

Celia passes by the Hotel Inglaterra, drab and peeling from neglect. Celia imagines her dead husband staring up at the shuttered windows, carrying a late-model electric broom. He studies the ornate balconies like a burglar, gazes through the blue panes of stained glass until he spots her with the

Spaniard, naked and sharing a cigarette. She imagines him swinging the broom round and round in a quickening circle, scattering pigeons and beggars, swinging so hard that the air breaks in a low whistle, swinging and swinging, then releasing the broom until it flies high above him, crashing through the window and shattering her past.

CELIA HITCHHIKES TO the Plaza de la Revolución, where El Líder, wearing his customary fatigues, is making a speech. Workers pack the square, cheering his words that echo and collide in midair. Celia makes a decision. Ten years or twenty, whatever she has left, she will devote to El Líder, give herself to his revolution. Now that Jorge is dead, she will volunteer for every project—vaccination campaigns, tutoring, the microbrigades.

In the back of the plaza, flatbed trucks are accepting volunteers for the fields. "There is no need to worry," El Líder assures them. "Work for the revolution today and tomorrow will take care of itself." Celia pulls on a hand stretched before her, its nails blunt and hard as hooves. A bottle of rum passes from mouth to mouth. Celia smooths her housedress then lifts the bottle. The liquor burns in her chest like a hot cloud.

For the next two weeks, Celia consigns her body to the sugarcane. From the trucks, the acres of cane are green and inviting. But deep in the fields the brownish stalks rise from the earth to more than twice her height, occluding her vision. There are rats everywhere, hollowing the sweetest stalks, and insects too numerous to swat. Celia learns to cut the cane straight across at the base, strip its leaves with her machete, then chop it in even pieces for the gatherers. Despite her age or because of it, Celia advances steadily through the fields, hardening her muscles with every step, every swing. She rips her hands on the tough, woody stalks. The sun browns her skin. Around her, the sugarcane hums.

One day, a worker slashes a volunteer with a machete. Celia stares as the blood mingles with the sweat of his victim's chest. "Amateurs!" the *machetero* shouts so everyone can hear. "Sunday peasants! Go to hell, all of you!" Several men grab the worker from behind and take him from the fields. Oblivious of the tumult, a Creole woman spits out a curse. Celia does not know to whom.

Celia imagines the cane she cuts being ground in the *centrales,* and its thick sap collected in vats. The furnaces will transform it to moist, amber crystals. She pictures three-hundred-pound sacks of refined white sugar deep in the hulls of ships. People in Mexico and Russia and Poland will spoon out her sugar for coffee, or to bake in their birthday cakes. And Cuba will grow prosperous. Not the false prosperity of previous years, but a prosperity that those with her on these hot, still mornings can share. Next season the cane will regenerate, a vegetal mystery, and she will return to cut it again. In another seven years, the fields will be burned and replanted.

In the evenings, the stink of sugarcane coats Celia's nostrils and throat, sweetening her meat and rice and the cigarettes she smokes. She soaks her feet in balms of herb water, plays cards past midnight, eats oranges under a full moon. She examines her hands daily with pride.

One dream recurs. A young girl in her Sunday dress and patent shoes selects shells along the shore, filling her limitless pockets. The sea retreats to the horizon, underlining the sky in a dark band of blue. Voices call out to the girl but she does not listen. Then the seas rush over her and she floats underwater with wide-open eyes. The ocean is clear as noon in winter. Bee hummingbirds swim alongside pheasants and cows. A mango sapling grows at her side. The fruits swell and burst crimson and the tree shrivels and dies.

WHEN CELIA RETURNS from the fields, she finds her daughter's condition has declined. Felicia's skin appears enameled in pinks like the wallpaper of Old Havana inns. The blue roses of her flannel nightgown adhere to her damp filth. Celia washes her daughter's hair over the kitchen sink then untangles it with a broken comb. She cannot persuade Felicia to take off her nightgown, to allow light in the tenebrous house.

"They stole my hair and sold it to the gypsies," Felicia complains. "The sun burns our imperfections."

"What are you talking about?" Celia asks impatiently.

"Light infiltrates. It's never safe."

"Please, *hija*, give me your gown to wash."

Felicia runs upstairs to her bed and lies with her hands tightly clasped under her breasts.

The twins complain that they've had nothing but ice cream to eat for days, that their mother dances with Ivanito and warns them of the dangers of daylight. Luz accuses Ivanito of repeating their mother's pretentious phrases, of saying things like "The moon glares with a vivid indifference."

"Come here, *chiquitico*," Celia coaxes, lifting her grandson to her lap. "I'm sorry I left you. I thought your mother would get better in a day or two."

Milagro touches a blister on her grandmother's palm. Celia displays her hands, marred by cuts and calluses. Her granddaughters explore the scarred terrain.

"Pack your bathing suits; we're going to Santa Teresa del Mar."

"I won't go!" Ivanito cries, and runs to bury himself in his mother's bed.

"Just for a few days. Your mother must rest," Celia calls after him. Suddenly she remembers her great-aunt's hands floating on a white surf of keys, overlapping like gulls in the air. Celia used to play duets with her Tía Alicia, side by side on the piano bench. Neighbors would stop and listen to the music, and occasionally invite themselves in for a cup of tea.

"You can't steal him," Felicia warns her mother, rocking Ivanito beneath the sheets.

CELIA LEADS THE twins away from the house on Palmas Street. The girls do not speak but their thoughts tumble together like gems in the polishing, reaching their hard conclusions. Celia fears their recollections—the smashed chairs that left splinters in their feet, the obscenities that hung like electric insects in the air.

Their father, Hugo Villaverde, had returned on several occasions. Once, to bring silk scarves and apologies from China. Another time to blind Felicia for a week with a blow to her eyes. Yet another, to sire Ivanito and leave his syphilis behind.

Despite this, Luz and Milagro insisted on keeping their father's name. Even after he left for good. Even after Felicia reverted to using her maiden name. The girls, Celia realized, would never be del Pinos.

Celia sits in the front seat of the bus with her granddaughters. As they leave Havana, a brisk rain falls, rattling the tin bus. Celia cannot mourn for her husband, she doesn't know why. She loved him, that she learned once, but the grief still won't come. What separates her from sorrow, she wonders. Felicia's delusions? The fortnight in the sugarcane fields? The swelter of the afternoon rains? Had she simply grown too accustomed to Jorge's absence?

Already it seems a long time since her husband walked on water in his white summer suit and Panama hat. Much longer still since he'd boarded the plane for New York.

Consuelo Hermer and Marjorie May

WHAT TO WEAR

TURISTA IS THE Cuban epithet of derision for everything gauche or socially incorrect. "*Turista!*" uttered with a what-else-can-you-expect shrug of the shoulders, is the Cuban's answer to all *faux pas* committed by visitors. Nothing stamps one as a *turista* more irrevocably than the wrong clothes. There isn't a more forlorn spectacle than a boatload of tourists descending upon

Consuelo Hermer's husband gave her and Marjorie May the idea to write Havana Mañana, *which was published in 1941. May, born in 1911, lived in Cuba for ten years as a child; to this date she claims: "I can still rhumba with a glass of water on my head."*

the Prado in January, decked out in the white linens, the Panama hats and all the Southern trappings foisted upon their unsuspecting persons by the resort departments of home-town shops. They are considerably baffled (that's understatement!) to find the Cubans conservatively going about in dark street clothes, business suits, suede shoes, felt hats—just the clothes the tourists left behind. Unpredictable as their own weather, Cubans are creatures of habit about dress. No matter how the mercury soars, from December through March (Cuban winter), dark clothes are worn. True, these are of tropical worsted or gabardine for men, and thin silk or rayon crepe for women; nevertheless, designs and colors are the same as fashions worn on Fifth Avenue during similar months.

Obviously, all of us choose the vacation clothes that look best and do most for us. Be sure, however, to figure out a wardrobe that is not at complete odds with the Cuban scene. Besides looking better, there's a perfectly practical reason for blending with your Havana environment. Looking as though you belong helps you to escape the plague of street peddlers and beggars that descends upon *turistas.* It is really a form of protective coloring.

Warning to the let-yourself-go school of thought: Don't even dare to think of wearing slacks, short socks or backless sun dresses in the city streets, if you're a woman; cork helmets or two-piece play ensembles, if you're a man. You'd never dream of walking down Broadway in such a get-up, would you? Remember that Havana is as large a city as San Francisco, and certainly as cosmopolitan. To dress as you would for the streets at home is your safest bet.

The Cuban summer begins April 1st, and overnight everyone changes into light colors. Now the men appear in magnificent hundred-twist linen drill suits, laundered and starched to the high perfection of fine damask tablecloths, while the women wear the same kind of warm-weather frocks seen on our city streets during the dog days. Again, your cue is to dress as you would for summer at home.

It is in the beach- and play-clothes department, how-ever, that you can really go to town! As long as you wear them at the right time and place—for active sports, on beaches, at private clubs—your play clothes can rival Joseph's coat. Women can play siren-on-the-sands and men disport themselves in the vivid trunks they have been too shy to wear before. Cubans adore novelties for sports, and a pair of rocking-chair heel sandals, fresh from Bonwit's, made one of us the sensation at the yacht club!

You're not going to wear evening clothes as much as you think you are; so go light on quantity. Cubans usually dress formally for public appearances only on Thursday and Saturday nights, or when something special is scheduled. Otherwise, evening kit is confined to private parties and club galas except during the Christmas holiday season. Then everything is particularly festive, and to dress is the rule rather than the exception.

FOR MEN ONLY: Many travelers fondly imagine casual clothes are all Havana requires. Nothing could be further from the truth. Native men are as clothes-conscious as their women, and the well-to-do take great pains with their wardrobes, achieving the results associated with elegant Continentals. Men of means naturally order their suits tailored to measure in the strictest European tradition, and their understanding of fabrics and needling gives them an almost feminine interest in dressing. Besides, everywhere one turns there are the military men; the army, the navy, the police, even the private night-watchmen, are in stunning uniforms, colorful as any from a musical comedy, fitting with whittled-down perfection. Really, they steal the show.

There is great adoration of American clothes, primarily because our mass-manufacturing methods supply such good-looking, well-fitting suits, ready-made. Also, our easy cut and fit do more to flatter the average male physique.

Cubans in lower-income brackets often indulge in extreme tailoring, trousers that fit too tightly, sporty-plus jackets, elaborate shoes with pointed toes. Your gentleman of income, however, is conservatively correct and wears boots in the best British manner, glossy and deeply polished. Almost all men have their shoes made to order, since prices for custom-made shoes are much lower than ours. Twelve dollars buys the finest leather and best workmanship.

Color is exciting to Cubans of every class. If they err in taste, it will be by wearing florid shades or combining too many. The Parisian love of detail and intricate fabrics is also quite Cuban, and the most common fashion blind-spot is in the failure to ensemble properly. Even the well-dressed Cuban sometimes gets himself together like a swing-band, each item of his apparel being chosen for its ability to hit a note and carry it. Evidently to his eye the individual merit of a shirt or tie is more important than its effect on the whole.

The suits an American takes to Cuba should be similar to those he'd wear at home, though lighter in weight. From December through March, tropical worsteds, gabardines, flannel slacks and tweed jackets in dark colors are best, accompanied by a light top-coat, of course, and a felt hat.

You will definitely need a hat for Havana; so don't be rash enough to run the risk of sun-stroke, notwithstanding shaded sidewalks. Incidentally, here, for once, are men whose hats are above reproach. Cubans not only have the knack of picking a good-looking felt, but one that actually flatters the face under it. And the well-dressed Cuban has many more hats than his American brother.

Be sure you have plenty of shirts, socks, underclothes and handkerchiefs; you will want to change more often than you do at home. If you have a yen for color, by all means, let yourself go in your ties. "The brighter, the better" is the Cuban's motto, and, currently, those big patterns are considered quite the thing.

Reiteration: We can't sufficiently deplore the bad taste shown by so many Americans who loom across hotel lobbies in messy, unpressed lounge suits, notable for un-chic. If you insist on disregarding our suggestion about sticking to fairly citified clothes in the large metropolis of Havana, we urge that your play clothes be unobtrusive in color and classic in style. For Heaven's sake, find a fabric blessed with enough stamina to hold its shape and not go baggy. When you wear such an outfit into a restaurant or hotel, slip on a jacket.

For evening, when dressing is in order, black dinner suits of tropical worsted are fine. Light jackets are a mistake during the winter season. Remember, however, that Cubans don't wear evening clothes in public as much as we do, and there isn't a night club doing business in Havana that will refuse admission to a cash customer because he's in street clothes.

When the summer season starts, everyone goes into whites, topped off with Panama hats, and March 31st sees Cuban business men carefully carrying home important-looking paper packages—their new straw hats. From April on, bring with you the best-looking linen and light-colored tropical-weight suits you can find. As we mentioned before, the Cubans are supreme in whites. They often have as many as six or seven white linen suits, change them after one wearing and look immaculate and fresh. For evening you can sport the same gray, white or beige jackets they affect, worn with cummerbunds.

When you pack your bathing suit, remember that *La Playa* (public beach) and some of the more conservative clubs require that men wear tops. And take along a sweat-shirt or robe as protection from too much sun.

WOMEN'S AND MISSES' DEPARTMENT: In Havana, the fashion tendency is all toward formality. No Cuban woman just puts on a dress and goes out. When she appears one is conscious of a toilette that makes an effect. She is preceded and followed by an almost tangible air of elegance, distinctly European in feeling. If she is wealthy, her costumes are either imported, with an abundance of intricate detail and fine hand-work, or custom-made. Because the *criolla* figure, like the Frenchwoman's, is short-limbed, her clothes must be fitted with extreme care, and to-order fashions rather than ready-made solve the problem of smarter Cubans.

If you find while you're in Havana that you want the fun of a new dress, provided time allows, you can have a knockout, made-to-order costume at much below U.S. cost. First, find your fabric. All the big stores have excellent yard-goods departments specializing in prints. If you want to snoop for bargains, there are shops along Muralla or Neptuno Streets that sell remnants of dress lengths. Now, what you need is that little dream of a dressmaker. Ask the salesgirl who sold you the silk or the cigar-counter girl or the manicurist. Somewhere along the line, you'll have success. Male or female, the dressmaker will carry out your ideas, copy a magazine sketch or design something especially for you, all very expertly and without benefit of pattern. You'll pay in the neighborhood of $10.00 or less, all told, for a typical couturier affair, cut to measure and worked out in canvas, first. Your frock will be completely individual in style, finished like an American outfit of fairly fabulous price. The well-known dressmakers along the Prado, however, price their creations much higher; don't expect to find bargains in any couturier-like establishment.

Part of the fun you'll get from your stay is the fuss that will be made over the details of your own appearance. You can expect to be subjected to a minute scrutiny every step of the way, from the girl behind the magazine counter who asks you what you do for your skin, to your Cuban escort who goes mad with joy because (thanks to God and Saks Fifth Avenue) your shoes show "the little fingers of the feet." Everyone loves American styles, and American residents may even attempt to buy your new bathing-suit right off your back! Try to take along at least one spanking-new fashion idea that has just appeared in the States. It will prove to be a great attention-getter and conversational ice-breaker. Just a silly gadget like a street-lamp lapel pin can start you on the royal road to success.

Be resigned in advance to the fact that the climate takes out your wave and simplify your hair-do before you leave home. (Suggestion from the Voice of Experience: Brilliantine is a life-saver in keeping unruly hair under control in this humid atmosphere.) Don't be timid about using the beauty shops in Havana. The operators usually are extremely competent and the prices, except at smart hotels, are lower than ours. We liked the way they fixed us up at El Encanto, and The America, on Calle San Miguel, does excellent work inexpensively.

Being "done" at a Cuban beauty shop is an interesting experience. The French technique, slow and painstaking, is employed, and your operator will fuss with your hair for ages. Dissuade her from designing a new coiffure, or from any other interesting experiments, else you may wind up like the old lady in the nursery rhyme, "Lord-a-mercy, can this be I?" . . . One of us misguidedly permitted the manicurist at the beach club to "put a little color" at the nails. What was it? A red rim around the cuticle!

The beautiful hair of Cuban women will impress you. They lacquer its natural luxuriance with brilliantine, devoting endless hours to keeping it in sleek perfection or designing new effects. The pageboy bob is widely worn but with personalized toprolls, coxcombs and fringes that make each head appear completely individual. The younger girls have gone overboard in favor of snoods because, besides being becoming, they keep hair-do's so nicely under control.

There is a different approach to the cosmetic question for you here, too. Come prepared to gild the lily. Havana's languorous beauties put you on your mettle. You will indulge in heavier eyeshadow, rouge, lipstick and mascara, heightening the *femme fatale* effect and achieving a generally more exotic appearance than you do in the States. It is really a psychological necessity, an effort not to seem pallid by comparison with the tropical sun and scenery. You will use more perfume, too, and probably adopt the native custom of dousing yourself liberally with toilet water for coolness as well as glamour.

The water is harder in Havana; so a water softener will make your baths more enjoyable. Remember that there is a Five-and-Ten easily accessible where you can stock up on invisibles or curlers or any other gadgets that were overlooked.

HEAD-TO-TOE WARDROBE GUIDE

SHOES: Include Old Faithful, a comfortable pair of low-heeled walking shoes. The rest can be fairly dressy, geared to other accessories, of course. Lightweight sandals are a smart choice, in fabric or straw. Keep away from patent leather or alligator;

they're hot. Incidentally, don't be alarmed if your ankles and legs get puffy. It's dat ole debil, tropical climate. The proper remedy is cold epsom-salt foot baths. When you rest, keeping your feet up higher than your head will help too.

HOSIERY: Take plenty because silk hose are quite high-priced in Havana and not comparable in quality to ours, at the prices charged. Nylons are ideal. Besides being magically long-lived, they don't insulate at all. After a long, hot day, there's none of the clammy stickiness you find with hose of natural silk. In the summer buy those thin toe and heel coverers of fresh lisle at Woolworth's, and forget about stockings completely if your legs are shapely, tanned and well-groomed.

LINGERIE: Take enough for many changes and be sure it is lightweight and porous. Laundry costs a pretty penny at hotels; so if you're smart you'll indulge in glove silks that can be rinsed out in a whisk and need no ironing. Foundations are a bit ornery in this climate. We recommend panty-girdles of mesh elastic and net or lace bras.

CLOTHES: Stick to a simple, one-color-scheme, basic wardrobe. From November through March, deep tones are smartest; lighter neutrals and bright shades come into their own for April to October. Citified prints with small decisive patterns on dark grounds are excellent. Dresses of silk jersey are a joy. They pack superbly, never wrinkle, always give that fresh-from-a-bandbox effect sometimes hard to achieve when you're living out of suitcases. Ring in as many changes of accessories as possible with special attention to jewelry and gadgets. A dark dress with a few sets of lingerie-type collars and cuffs is always good.

For a week's stay you will need a minimum of two street dresses, three afternoon frocks and one evening gown. If you're going to the beach often or expect to spend time in the country, include a casual spectator costume. Your coat can be spring weight, preferably a monotone wool that will harmonize with everything. For evening, take a short wrap, one that can double for daytime wear too. If your visit is to extend past a week, bring as many changes as possible. You'll be seeing the same people, visiting the same spots; so clothes variety will be the spice of your life.

If you're staying at Rio Cristal, the Country Club, or planning an expedition to Varadero, gay beach pajamas or slack suits are a necessity. Cuban women rarely wear shorts, except for active sports, perhaps because they're not too flattering. As a matter of fact, at Varadero, you don't need dresses at all. From morning to night, natives wear the brightest pajama ensembles they can find and load on multiple strands of the tiny shell necklaces peddled all over the place. The result is colorful as well as comfortable.

Your bathing suit should be as startling as your figure can stand, and unless you have tough skin, be sure to take a broad-brimmed beach hat to protect you from the sun and glare.

HATS: As many as possible is the idea, and they should be gay and eye-catching. Veils are highly appreciated. Incidentally, you'll notice that some of the older Cuban ladies go hatless with veils tied over their faces and hair—a lingering of the *mantilla* epoch. *Mantillas* are still in evidence at formal occasions. In the summer, Cuban women don't wear hats at all. Unless you want a big brim for shade, you'll find hats a nuisance. Bring instead scarves and kerchiefs that can be twisted into turbans. They're effective and far more comfortable.

FURS: Paradoxically enough, there's a big furore over furs in Havana. The great silver-fox plague raging up North has now spread down to the tropics. Cuban women of means adore mink, ermine, sable, fox, all the precious furs, and wear them lavishly. As a matter of fact, Havana seems to be a Mecca for phony furs among the poorer women. To own a fur-piece is everyone's ambition, even if it's only a skimpy one-skin scarf of dubious ancestry. So if you're on tour during the winter season, bring your little furs: scarves, stoles, capes or jackets of lightweight pelts.

ACCESSORIES: Make your main effect with lots of frivolous incidentals: jewelry, scarves, belts, flowers and gadgets. Forget about gloves completely; you'll never use them. Have at least one capacious carry-all pocketbook, the kind with a zipper pocket for travelers' checks and other state papers. Your dress bag should be as smart and sumptuous-looking as possible. Remember, it's going to be lying on tables in full view of critical Cuban eyes. And you'll need an evening bag, too.

Havana is one place where you can indulge your love for the ornamental. Prettiness and femininity are favored here, and anything that helps achieve this effect is all to the good. Fans are still used with much coquetry. Lorgnettes are everyday equipment, for no Cuban woman would dream of hiding her beautiful eyes behind spectacles, no matter how badly she needed them. In the summer you can even carry a lacy parasol without exciting anything but admiring comment.

Last warning: Pristine white accessories out of season are the unfailing identification mark of lady *turistas!*

Fidel Castro

CUBAN CHILDHOOD

BETTO: LET'S START with your background. You come from a Christian family.

Castro: Well, before I reply, now that you've provided an introduction, I'd like to explain that, knowing you were interested in an interview on this complex and delicate topic, I would have liked to have had more time to review some materials and give some thought to the matter. However, since the interview has coincided with a period of

Fidel Castro was born in 1926 in the easternmost part of Cuba to a farmer and his mistress. Early on he became heavily involved in politics, which ultimately led to his becoming leader of Cuba in 1959. Castro discussed his roots with Frei Betto in Fidel and Religion *(1987).*

intense work for both of us and with your pressing need to return to your country, I agreed to discuss all these topics in a practically impromptu manner. It reminds me of a student who has to take an exam but hasn't had time to study the subject, or a speaker who has to deliver a speech but hasn't had the opportunity to familiarize himself a great deal with the topic and deepen his understanding of it, or a teacher who has to give a class without having had even a minute to review the subject matter. It is in these circumstances that I embark on this conversation.

I know that this is a topic you have mastered thoroughly. You have the edge on me. You've studied theology extensively, and you've also studied Marxism a great deal. I know some Marxism and really very little about theology. I know that your questions and statements will be serious and profound and that, even though I'm not a theologian but rather a politician—I also believe I'm a revolutionary politician who has always been very frank about everything—I will try to answer all your questions with absolute honesty.

You say that I come from a religious family. How can I respond to such a statement? I could say, first, that I come from a religious nation and, second, that I come from a religious family. At least my mother was a very religious woman, a deeply religious woman—more religious than my father was.

Betto: Was your mother from the countryside?

Castro: Yes.

Betto: Cuban?

Castro: Yes, from a farm family.

Betto: And your father?

Castro: My father too came from a farm family. He was a very poor farmer from Galicia, Spain.

However, I wouldn't say that my mother was religious because she'd received any religious training.

Betto: Did she have faith?

Castro: There's no doubt that she had a great deal of faith, and I'd like to add that she learned how to read and write when she was practically an adult.

Betto: What was her name?

Castro: Lina.

Betto: And your father's?

Castro: Angel.

My mother was practically illiterate. She learned how to read and write all by herself. I don't remember her ever having a teacher other than herself. She never mentioned one. With great effort, she tried to learn. I never heard of her ever having gone to school. She was self-taught. She couldn't attend school or church or receive religious training. I think her religious beliefs had their origin in some family tradition, for her parents—especially her mother, my grandmother—were also very religious.

Betto: Was this religiousness limited to the home, or did she attend church frequently?

Castro: Well, it couldn't involve frequent church attendance, because there wasn't any church where I was born, far from any city.

Betto: Where were you born?

Castro: In the north-central part of what used to be Oriente Province, near Nipe Bay.

Betto: What was the name of the town?

Castro: Well, it wasn't a town. There was no church; it wasn't a town.

Betto: Was it a farm?

Castro: Yes, a farm.

Betto: And it was called—

Castro: Birán. It had a few buildings. There was the family house, and an annex containing a few small offices had been built on at one corner. Its architectural lines could be described as Spanish. You may wonder why a house built in Cuba should have Spanish architecture. It was because my father was a Spaniard, from Galicia. In the villages there, they had the custom of working a plot of land and keeping their animals under the house during the winter or in general. They raised pigs and kept some cows there. That's why I said my house was based on Galician architecture, because it was built on stilts.

Betto: Why? As protection against floods?

Castro: No, there really wasn't any need for that,

because there wasn't any flooding. Coincidentally, many years later, the blueprints that were drawn up in Cuba for the junior high schools in the countryside—very modern, solid buildings—called for piles, but not for the same reason. The idea was to eliminate the need for earth-moving operations to level the ground. Using a series of support columns in areas where the land sloped saved on such operations. Cement piles of different lengths were used to achieve a level base.

I've often wondered why my house had such tall stilts. Some of them were more than six feet high. The land under the house was uneven, so that, at the far end of the house, where the kitchen was located in an extension attached to the house, the stilts were shorter. At the other end, there was a slight inclination, and they were taller. But, as I've already explained, this wasn't so because of a desire to economize on earth moving. Even though, as a child, I never stopped to think about such things, I'm convinced it was because of the Galician custom. Why? Because I remember that, when I was very young—about three, four, five or maybe six years old—

the cows used to sleep under the house. There were from 20 to 30 of them, and they were rounded up at dusk and driven to the house, where they slept below. They were milked there, and some were tied to the stilts.

I forgot to tell you that the house was made of wood. No mortar, cement or bricks. Plain wood. The stilts were made of hardwood, and they served as the foundation for the floor. It was a one-story house, and I imagine it was originally square. It was lengthened later on with the addition of a passage leading from one side of the house to several small rooms. The first room had cabinets where medicines were kept; it was called the medicine room. The next one was the bathroom. Then came a small pantry, followed by a hallway that led to the dining room and finally the kitchen. Between the dining room and the kitchen, there was a flight of stairs leading down to the ground. Another addition was made later on. A sort of office was built onto one corner. So, it was a square house on stilts with those additions. By the time I began to notice things around me, the kitchen had already been built. Above the square portion, there was another floor called the lookout, where my parents and their first three children slept until I was four or five years old.

Betto: Did your mother have any religious statues?

Castro: Yes, I'm going to talk about that, but first I want to finish with the Spanish countryside architecture and other details.

My father built the house in keeping with the customs of his native region. He also had a farm background and didn't have any opportunity to study. So, like my mother, he learned how to read and write all by himself, through sheer determination.

My father was the son of a very poor farmer in Galicia. At the time of Cuba's last War of Independence, which began in 1895, he was sent here as a Spanish soldier, to fight. So, here my father was, very young and drafted into military service as a soldier in the Spanish Army. When the war was over, he was shipped back to Spain, but it seems he'd taken a liking to Cuba. Along with many other immigrants, he left for Cuba in the early years of this century. Penniless and with no relatives here, he got himself a job.

Important investments were made in that period. U.S. citizens had seized the best land in Cuba and had started to destroy forests, build sugar mills and grow sugarcane, all of which involved big investments in those days. My father worked in one of the sugar mills.

Betto: When did the War of Independence take place?

Castro: The last War of Independence began in 1895 and ended in 1898. Spain had been virtually defeated when the United States staged its opportunistic intervention in that war. It sent soldiers; took over Puerto Rico, the Philippines and some other islands in the Pacific; and occupied Cuba. It couldn't seize Cuba permanently, because Cuba had been fighting for a long time. Even though their numbers were small, the Cuban people had been fighting heroically for many years. The United States didn't plan to seize Cuba openly, because the cause of Cuba's independence had extensive support in Latin America and the world as a whole. As I have repeatedly said, Cuba was the nineteenth century's Vietnam.

As I was saying, my father returned to Cuba and began working. Later, he apparently got a group of workers together. He managed them and contracted the men to work for a U.S. firm. He set up a sort of small enterprise that, as far as I can remember, cleared land to plant sugarcane or felled trees to supply sugar mills with firewood. It's possible that, as the organizer of that enterprise with a group of men under him, he began to make a profit. In other words, my father was clearly a very active, enterprising person, and he had an instinctive sense of organization.

I don't know very much about the early years, because, when I had a chance to inquire, I wasn't as curious as I am now about what my father did after reaching the age of reason. I couldn't do with him what you're doing with me, and, now, who could tell us about his experiences?

Betto: When did your father die?

Castro: Much later, when I was 32. He died in 1956, before I came back from Mexico on the *Granma* expedition.

Now, allow me to finish up these details before answering your question.

Betto: I thought you were 32 when the Revolution triumphed in January 1959.

Castro: Well, I was 32. I turned 33 in August 1959.

Betto: But, if he died in 1956, then you were even younger—about 30 years old.

Castro: That's right. You're absolutely right. I forgot to include the two years of the war. The war lasted two years—25 months, to be exact. My father died on October 21, 1956, two months after my thirtieth birthday. In December 1956, when I came back from Mexico with my small expedition, I was 30. I was 26 when we attacked the Moncada Garrison, and I spent my twenty-seventh birthday in prison.

Betto: And your mother; when did she die?

Castro: On August 6, 1963, four and a half years after the triumph of the Revolution.

I was about to finish your earlier point. Your questions have diverted me from the topic. We were talking about the countryside, where we lived, what the house was like, what my parents were like and the educational level they had achieved in spite of their very poor background. I told you all about the house and how it had incorporated Spanish traditions.

I can't really remember many indications of my father's being a religious person. I'd say there were very few of them. I couldn't even say whether or not he really had any religious faith, but I do remember that my mother was very religious, just like my grandmother.

Betto: Did he go to Mass on Sundays, for example?

Castro: I already told you there wasn't any church where we lived.

Betto: How was Christmas celebrated in your house?

Castro: In the traditional way. Christmas Eve was a time for celebration. Then came New Year's Eve, which involved a party that would go on till past midnight. I think there was also a religious holiday on the day of *Santos Inocentes* (Holy Innocents' Day), which I think was celebrated on December 28. The custom was to play tricks on people, to pull their leg or tell them some tall tale, and say, "Fooled you, didn't I?" That was also part of the Christmas season.

Betto: In Brazil, that day is April 1.

Castro: Well, here it was the end of the year. Christmas was celebrated, as was Holy Week.

However, I still haven't answered your first question as to whether or not my family was religious.

There was no town—only a few buildings—where we lived. When I was a child, the cows were kept under the house. Later, they were moved somewhere else. In addition, there was always a small pen with pigs and poultry under the house, just like in Galicia. The place was inhabited by hens, ducks, guinea hens, turkeys, some geese and pigs—all kinds of domestic animals. Later, a barn was built around 30 or 40 meters away from the house. A small slaughterhouse was close by, and there was a small smithy, where tools, plows and other farm implements were repaired, in front of the bar. The bakery was around 30 or 40 meters away from the house in a different direction. The elementary school—a small public school—was around 60 meters from the house on the other side of the bakery, next to the main road. That mud and dirt road, which was called a highway, ran south from the municipal capital. The general store—the commercial center—was also owned by my family and had a leafy tree in front. The post office and telegraph office were opposite the store. Those were the main facilities there.

Betto: Your family owned the store?

Castro: Yes, but not the post office or the little schoolhouse. They were public property. All the rest belonged to my family. By the time I was born, my father had already accumulated resources, a certain degree of wealth.

Betto: When were you born?

Castro: On August 13, 1926. If you want to know the time, I think it was around 2:00 in the morning. Maybe that had something to do with my guerrilla spirit, with my revolutionary activities. Nature and the time of my birth must have had some influence. There are other factors that should be taken into account now, right—what kind of day it was and whether or not Nature has anything to do with the lives of men. Anyway, I think I was born early in the morning—I think I was told that once. Therefore, I was born a guerrilla, because I was born at around 2:00 in the morning.

Betto: Yes, part of a conspiracy.

Castro: A bit of a conspiracy.

Betto: At least the number 26 seems to have had quite a bearing on your life.

Castro: Well, I was born in 1926; that's true. I was 26 when I began the armed struggle, and I was born on the thirteenth, which is half of 26. Batista staged his coup d'etat in '52, which is twice 26. Now that I think of it, there may be something mystical about the number 26.

Betto: You were 26 when you began the struggle. The attack on the Moncada was on the 26th of July, and it gave rise to the 26th of July Movement.

Castro: And we landed in 1956, which is the round number of 30 plus 26.

Well, Betto, allow me to continue, because I still haven't answered your question.

I've been telling about what we had on the farm, but there's something else. The pit for cockfights was around 100 meters from the house, on the main road. During the sugar harvest, cockfights were held there every Sunday—cockfights, not bullfights. In Spain, there would have been both, but what I saw there were cockfights every Sunday, on December 25, around New Year's time and every holiday. The cockfighting fans would gather there, and some of them brought their own fighting cocks. Others limited themselves to betting. Many poor people lost their small incomes there. When they lost, they went home broke; when they won, they immediately spent the money on rum and parties.

Not far from the pit, there were some poor dwellings, huts made of palm thatch with dirt floors. Most of them were inhabited by Haitian immigrants who worked on the farms and in the planting and cutting of sugarcane. They'd come to Cuba early in the twentieth century and led a miserable existence. Even way back then, there were Haitian immigrants in Cuba. It seems the work force in Cuba wasn't large enough, which is why Haitian immigrants came. The huts where the workers and their families lived were all over the place—along the main road and other roads, including the one that led to the railway that was used to transport the sugarcane, and even alongside the tracks.

The farm's main crop was sugarcane. Cattle was next, and, after that, truck farming. There were bananas, root vegetables, small plots planted with cereals, some vegetables, coconut trees and various fruit trees; there was a 10- to 12-hectare citrus grove near the house. The cane fields were farther away, closer to the railroad line that was used to take the sugarcane to the sugar mill.

By the time I started to take note of my surroundings, my family owned some land and leased some more. How much land did my father own? I'll tell you in hectares, even though we measure land in *caballerías* in Cuba. One *caballería* is equal to 13.4 hectares. My father owned around 800 hectares of land.

Betto: Is the Cuban hectare similar to the Brazilian one?

Castro: A hectare is a square each of whose sides is 100 meters long—that is, 10,000 square meters.

Betto: Ten thousand square meters, exactly.

Castro: That's a hectare.

Apart from that, my father leased some land. It wasn't as good as the land he owned, but it covered a much larger area, around 10,000 hectares.

Betto: Commander, that's a lot of land in Brazil. Just imagine—

Castro: Well, he'd leased all that land. Most of it was hilly, with steep slopes, large areas densely wooded with pine trees and a plateau at an altitude of 700 to 800 meters. Up there, the soil is red and there are large deposits of nickel and other metals. The Revolution has reforested that area. I liked that plateau very much, because it was cool. When I was around 11 years old, I used to go there on horseback. The horses had to struggle, climbing up the steep hillsides, but once they got there, they'd stop sweating and be dry in a matter of minutes. It was marvelously cool up there, because a breeze was always blowing through the tall, dense pine trees, whose tops met, forming a kind of roof. The water in the many brooks was ice-cold, pure and delicious. That whole area was leased. It didn't belong to the family.

Several years later, the family's income grew with a new asset: lumber. Some of the land that my father had leased included forested areas that were exploited for the lumber. Other sections consisted of hills where cattle were raised, and another part was used for raising sugarcane and other agricultural crops.

Betto: So your father rose from being a poor farmer to a landowner.

Castro: I have a photo of the house in Galicia where my father was born. It was very small, about the size of this room—from 10 to 12 meters long and from 6 to 8 meters wide. It was made of stone, which was abundant in the area and was often used by the farmers for the construction of their rustic dwellings. That was the house where the family lived. A one-room house combining bedroom and kitchen. I imagine there were animals too. The family didn't own any land—not even a square meter.

In Cuba, he bought around 800 hectares of land and leased some more, from some veterans of the War of Independence. It would take a good deal of research, delving into history, to find out how these veterans of the War of Independence came to own 10,000 hectares of land. Of course, those two veterans had been high-ranking officers in the War of Independence. I never thought about doing any research on the matter, but I imagine it was easy for them to get it. There was plenty of land at the time, and, in one way or another—perhaps by paying a very low price for it—they managed to buy it. People from the United States bought extensive tracts of land at very low prices, but I can't imagine what money or other resources those veterans had that enabled them to buy the land. Afterwards, they got a percentage from the sale of the sugarcane that was grown there, plus a percentage from the sale of the lumber that was taken from their forests. They had independent means, lived in Havana and had other businesses on the side. I can't really say whether those people got title to that land legally or illegally.

That vast extent of land was of two types: the land that my father owned and the land that he leased.

How many people lived on that vast latifundium at that time? Hundreds of workers' families; many of them worked small plots that my father let them have so they could grow crops for their own consumption. There were also some farmers who grew sugarcane, who were known as *subcolonos*. Their situation wasn't as difficult as the workers'. How many families were there in all? Two hundred, maybe 300; when I was around 11 years old, around 1000 people lived in that vast area.

I thought it would be useful to explain all these things in order to give you an idea of the environment in which I was born and raised.

There wasn't a single church, not even a small chapel.

Betto: Nor did a priest ever visit the place.

Castro: No, a priest used to show up once a year for baptisms. The area where I lived belonged to a municipality called Mayarí, and a priest used to come from the municipal seat, 36 kilometers away by the highroad.

Batto: Were you baptized there?

Castro: No; I was baptized in Santiago de Cuba, several years after I was born.

Betto: How old were you then?

Castro: I think I was around five or six. I was one of the last children in my family to be baptized.

Let me explain something: in that place, there was no church, no priests and no religious training whatsoever. Before going into the story of my baptism, I want to make it clear that there was no such thing as religious training there.

You asked me if those hundreds of families were believers. I'd say that, generally speaking, they were. As a rule, everybody there had been baptized. I remember that those who hadn't been baptized were called Jews. I couldn't understand what the term *Jew* meant—I'm referring to the time when I was four or five years old. I knew it was a very noisy, dark-colored bird, and every time somebody said, "He's a Jew," I thought they were talking about that bird. Those were my first impressions. Anyone who hadn't been baptized was a "Jew."

There was no religious training. The school was a small, nondenominational school. About 15 to 20 children went there. I was sent there because there wasn't any nursery school. I was the third-oldest child in my family, and my nursery school was that school. They sent me there when I was very young. They didn't have anything else to do with me, so they sent me there with my older sister and brother.

I can't even remember when I learned how to read and write. All I remember is that they used to put me in a small desk in the front row, where I could see the blackboard and listen to everything that was being said. So, it may be said that I learned in nursery school—which was the school. I think it was there that I learned reading, writing and arithmetic. How old was I then? Probably four, or maybe five.

Religion wasn't taught in that school. You were taught the national anthem and told about the flag, the coat of arms and things like that. It was a public school.

Those families had different kinds of beliefs. I remember what people in the countryside thought about religion. They believed in God and also in a number of saints. Some of those saints were in the Liturgy; they were official saints. Others weren't. Everybody had his own saint, after whom he was named. You were told that your saint's day was very important, and you were very happy when it rolled around. April 24 was my saint's day, because there's a saint called Fidel. There was another saint before me, I want you to know.

Mario Puzo and Francis Coppola

THE GODFATHER II

EXT. VIEW FROM BOAT – FULL VIEW – DAY

A beautiful coastal view of a tropical Caribbean city. An extraordinary view, high buildings, palm trees, all set right on the bay.

MED. CLOSE VIEW ON MICHAEL on the cruiser, Bussetta

When Francis Ford Coppola was first approached about directing The Godfather, *he read fifty pages of Mario Puzo's best-seller, put it down, and proclaimed it "a popular, sensational novel, pretty cheap stuff." Financial considerations forced him and Puzo to create the Hollywood classic.*

a little distance away, watching but never speaking. The dark-skinned CAPTAIN of the cruiser keeps pointing repeatedly.

CAPTAIN: Habana, Habana.

EXT. HAVANA STREET – MOVING VIEW – DAY
Michael and Bussetta are driven in a Mercury sedan, making its way through the streets of Havana.

CLOSE VIEW ON MICHAEL looking out the window.

MICHAEL'S POV Crowded streets, occasional roving bands playing for the tourists; there is much evidence of tourism: Americans walking through the streets with cameras. Occasionally, we see a Cuban with a row of numbers attached to his hat, carrying a big sheet of the daily lottery numbers. From all of these street impressions, the city is booming with activity, but there is also much evidence of whores and pimps and little children begging in the street.

MED. VIEW The big American car stops at an intersection. Bussetta is sitting in the forward passenger side; while Michael is in the back. He hears tapping on the window; he turns and sees four Cuban boys tapping on his window and extending their hands, and rubbing their stomachs as though they were hungry. The Cuban driver rolls down his window and shouts them away in Spanish.

INT. HAVANA CASINO LOBBY – MOVING VIEW – NIGHT Michael is led through a beautiful wooden lobby of the hotel, done in Spanish style, apparently just recently completed. He is approached by a thin, mousey man, SAM ROTH, who ushers him toward the casino entrance.

SAM ROTH: Hiya, Mr. Corleone, I'm Sam Roth. Welcome to the Capri; my brother's upstairs. You wanta take a rest before you see him, or can I get you something, anything at all?

MICHAEL: No, I'm fine.

> He leads Michael into the main casino.

SAM ROTH: This is it! We think it makes Vegas look like the corner crap game.

MICHAEL: Very impressive.

SAM ROTH: Jake, Jake, come over here. Mike, I want you to meet Jake Cohen; he manages the casino for us.

COHEN (appreciating Michael's status): Mr. Corleone.

> Sam turns to Bussetta and extends his glad-hand.

SAM ROTH: Pleasure to meet you, I'm sure . . .

> He gets no response whatsoever from Bussetta.

INT. PRESIDENTIAL PALACE – NIGHT An extremely tall, well-built Cuban, tanned and wearing an attractive mustache, LEON, in his middle forties, reads from a prepared paper. His sentences are translated by a smaller man, standing to his rear.

LEON (Spanish): Most respected gentlemen, allow me to welcome you to the City of Havana, the Republic of Cuba on behalf of His Excellency, Fulgencio Batista.

THE VIEW BEGINS TO MOVE along the various men gathered for this meeting.

LEON (o.s.): I'd like to thank this distinguished group of American Industrialists, for continuing to work with Cuba, for the greatest period of prosperity in her entire history. Mr. William Proxmire, representing The General Fruit Company . . . Messrs. Corngold and Dant, of the United Telephone and Telegraph Company; Mr. Petty, regional Vice-President of the Pan American Mining Corporation; and, of course, our good friend Mr. Robert Allen, of South

American Sugar. Mr. Nash of the American State Department. And Mr. Hyman Roth of Miami, and Michael Corleone of Nevada representing our Associates in Tourism and Leisure Activities.

VIEW ON THE ENTIRE GROUP Leon pauses to take a drink of water. Then proudly, he lifts a shiny yellow telephone for all to see.

LEON: The President would like to take this opportunity to thank U T&T for their lovely gift: a solid gold telephone! He thought all you gentlemen would care to take a look at it.

He hands the heavy phone set to one of his aides, and it is passed in turn to each of the men in attendance.

CORNGOLD OF UTT: Your Excellency, perhaps you could discuss the status of rebel activity and how this may affect our business.

MED. CLOSE VIEW ON MICHAEL He receives the telephone, and glances at it before passing it on to Hyman Roth.

LEON (o.s.): Of course. The rebel movement is basically unpopular, and since July of 1958 has been contained in the Oriente Province, in the mountains of the Sierra Muestre.

    Michael passes the phone on to Roth.

LEON (continuing): We began a highly successful offensive against them in March, and activities within the city itself are at a minimum. I can assure you we'll tolerate no guerrillas in the casinos or swimming pools!

    General subdued laughter.

A CUBAN STREET – LATE DAY Police are stopping traffic. Michael's Mercury is among the cars; a police officer, seeing that some important person is being driven, walks up to the driver. He leans forward, and says something in Spanish to the driver. The driver, in turn, leans over to Michael.

DRIVER: He says it will just be a short time and they'll let us through.

Michael looks out the window.

MICHAEL'S VIEW The old building has been totally sur-rounded by police and military vehicles. Right at this moment, they are waiting lazily, but soldiers are there with automatic weapons ready. There is a momentary commotion inside the building, and the men brace up. A Captain of the Army detach-ment says something in Spanish over a megaphone and his men put their weapons at the ready, as other policemen lead a group of civilians out of the building with their hands up.

They are moved over to some military truck, where they are frisked before being loaded.

All of a sudden, one of the civilian rebels breaks loose and rushes toward the command vehicle. He hurls himself into the vehicle, as two police try to pull him out. A second later, there is an explosion; the man obviously having hidden a grenade on his body, sacrificing his own life to take the life of the Captain.

There is a commotion, but the military quickly quell it.

CLOSE VIEW ON MICHAEL watching. The police rush to Michael's car and guide it outside of the trouble area.

MED. VIEW as they lead and escort the Mercury out of the area.

EXT. HAVANA COUNTRY CLUB – CLOSE VIEW – DAY Some glasses; rum is poured into them; then Coca Cola. Quarter limes are squeezed.

SAM ROTH (o.s.): Rum . . . Coca Cola . . . a squeeze of fresh lime . . .

Sam prepares the drinks for his brother, Hyman, and a group of men, including Michael.

A MAN: Cuba Libres.

MICHAEL: I was told the Cubans now call this drink: "La Mentira."

HYMAN ROTH: I still don't speak Spanish, Michael.

MICHAEL: It means . . . "The Lie."
A moment's hesitation, then a few of the men laugh. Now two Cubans in white carry a table which has a lovely small cake on it.

SAM ROTH: The cake is here.
    They all raise their glasses to the old man.

EVERYONE (ad lib): Happy Birthday!
    Roth glances at the cake and its inscription, is pleased.

HYMAN ROTH: I hope my age is correct: I am always accurate about my age.
    Some laugh. He nods, and they begin to cut it, put a piece on plates, and carry them to the different men.

HYMAN ROTH: Everything we've learned in Vegas is true here; but we can go further. The bigger, the swankier, the plusher the store, the more a sense of legitimacy, and the bigger business we do.

(looking at the plate brought to him)

A smaller piece. What we've proposed to the Cuban Government is that it put up half the cash on a dollar for dollar basis.

(accepting a smaller piece)

Thank you. We can find people in the United States who will put up our share for a small piece of the action, yet we will retain control.

ONE OF THE MEN: How much?

ROTH: A hundred million dollars. But only if this Government relaxes its restrictions on importing building materials; we'll need some new laws, too, but that will be no difficulty.

ANOTHER MAN: What are import duties now?

ROTH: As much as seventy per cent. Also, I'm working out an arrangement with the Minister of Labor so that all our pit bosses, stick-men and Dealers, can be considered specialized technicians eligible for two year visas. As of now they're only allowed in Cuba for six months at a time. In short, we're in full partnership with the Cuban Government.

VIEW ON MICHAEL is handed a piece of cake. Roth moves over to a folder of documents.

ROTH (continuing): Here are applications from Friends all over the States. I understand Santo Virgilio in Tampa is trying to make his own deal. Well, the Cuban Government will brush him off. The Lakeville Road Boys are going to take over the Nacionale here. I'm planning a new hotel casino to be known as Riviera. The new Capri will go to the Corleone Family.

MED. VIEW The cake is sliced and carried to each of the men.

ROTH: Then there's the Sevilla Biltmore; the Havana Hilton, which is going to cost twenty-four million — Cuban banks will put up half, the Teamsters will bankroll the rest. Generally, there will be friends for all our friends including the Lieutenant Governor of Nevada; Eddie Levine of Newport will bring in the Pennino Brothers, Dino and Eddie; they'll handle actual casino operations.

And seeing that all of his friends have been served, Roth raises his fork.

ROTH: Enjoy.

MICHAEL: I saw an interesting thing today. A man was being arrested by the Military Police; probably an urban guerrilla. Rather than be taken alive, he exploded a grenade hidden in his jacket, taking the command vehicle with him.

The various men look up as Michael eats his cake, wondering what the point of it is.

MICHAEL: It occurred to me: the police are paid to fight, and the Rebels are not.

SAM ROTH: So?

MICHAEL: So, that occurred to me.

VIEW ON ROTH He understands Michael's point, if the others do not.

HYMAN ROTH: This country has had rebels for the last fifty years; it's part of their blood. Believe me, I know . . . I've been coming here since the twenties; we were running molasses out of Havana when you were a baby. To trucks owned by your father. (he chuckles warmly over the memory)
We'll talk when we're alone.

    And he returns his attention to the men who are gathered with him on his birthday.

EXT. ROTH'S PRIVATE TERRACE — DAY Michael sits alone with the old man, on a terrace that overlooks the city.

ROTH: You have to be careful what you say in front of the others . . . they frighten easy. It's always been that way, most men frighten easy.

MICHAEL: We're making a big investment in Cuba. That's my only concern.

ROTH: My concern is that the three million never arrived at Batista's numbered account in Switzerland. He thinks it's because you have second thoughts about his ability to stop the rebels.

MICHAEL: The money was sent.

ROTH: Then you have to trace it. Michael, people here look at me as a reliable man. I can't afford not to be looked on as a reliable man. But you know all that; there's nothing you can learn from me. You shouldn't have to put up with a sick old man as a partner.

MICHAEL: I wouldn't consider anyone else.

ROTH: Except the President of the United States.

He laughs slyly, as though this is some private joke between them. Then his laughter becomes a cough, which he painfully stifles with a handkerchief.

Sophia Peabody Hawthorne

THE CUBA JOURNAL, 1834

San Marcos. La Recompenza. January 13. 1834.

MY DEAREST MOTHER,

This is but the third letter I have written to America.
Yesterday I sent the second to Maria Chase, to go by the brig
Dromo to new york, because I promised her she should have the

---

Sophia Peabody Hawthorne sailed to Cuba in 1833 to take a cure for debili-
tating headaches, probably brought on by an oppressive mother, and seemed to
improve the minute the shore passed over the horizon. After her return, she
married Nathaniel Hawthorne, who immortalized her as the character of
Phoebe in House of the Seven Gables.

second; but you will read it just the same, and I hope you have already received the first, which I wrote on board the New castle. Instead of writing such numbers of epistles in the vessel as I anticipated, I found I could do nothing but look abroad and dream and meditate. Every thing was so new, and glorious, and vast, that I could not fix my mind or eyes upon a sheet of paper, seldom upon a book, & the ocean was just as full of charm and novelty and interest the day we anchored in the harbour of Havana as on the day we sailed from Boston. I could not bear to leave it or our dear little world where we had all been so happy together. Mary was indefatigably industrious and dispatched books and pincushions the latter by the dozen, besides writing a journal constantly. I read the twentieth part of a book, a few stanzas of Child Harold, studied a little Spanish and made one pincushion! Oh yes, I marked one of the Captain's new table clothes with a T.H. which excited the admiration of the whole ship's company. I spied a great deal with the Captain's glass at distant ships and land when ever they were in sight. I saw the first Palm tree wave through the glass, which gave me a strange consciousness that I was approaching a foreign land. Our entrance into the harbour was beautiful. Moro Castle did not look as I thought; but it was very grand never the less. Two other vessels entered about the time we did from the United States, one containing Mr Curson, the other Mrs Williams. We were no sooner anchored than the government boats came out to us. The first was rowed by twelve men in livery at one end, and under an awning at the other sat the officers. The king's flag floated in the sea from a staff with a strip of bl. drape [?] in memory of his death. After this boat left us, the other came up, much less stylish, to enquire about the health of our vessels. We had hardly been there an hour before Mr Morland and a certain Mr Bruce suddenly appeared on deck. Horace had gone on shore in the first boat and immediately got us a permit from the governor, like a good boy. So before we could realize we had arrived we were sailing in a nice little green boat towards land, with Mr Morland and Mr Bruce. We stopped at the ship Mrs Williams came in, and took her with us. Two Spaniards rowed our boat, looking exquisitely nice and cool, dressed in white linen with

worked bosoms to their shirts. Mr M. said that Havana was perfectly healthy. So we Sprung upon the soil of Cuba with quite a
feeling of security. Mr Bruce took us under his arms and in a
very short time we were mounting the stone steps of Mr Cleveland's house. Mrs C. received us with open arms, with all the
warmth of her nature; but she was so dreadfully changed in
appearance that I felt really faint at seeing her. Mr Cleveland is
not so changed but looks much more feeble. His suite of rooms
is in the third story and extremely lofty, un ceiled, with stone
floors laid in diamonds. The drawing room is carpeted with
straw; but the hall is in a state of nature. The windows are all
very wide and high and open to the floor and lead out upon little
balconies. The custom house is on one side of the house, at the
gate of which two soldiers are perpetually on guard. There is a
very narrow peep at the bay from one window and the never
ceasing song of the negroes as they raise the sugar and coffee into
the ships is enough to create a slow fever. The street cries of men
and women with fruits upon their heads, the squalls of children,
the continuous stream of talk from groups all about, uttered in

the highest key, the monotonous hammering of coopers & tinkers the screams of macaws & parrots and all the unmusical birds that make a grand noise; the roarings and gibbering of a company of Catalans who occupy rooms under Mrs Cleveland's, almost put me beside myself. Add to all this gales, not "from Araby the blest" which obliges you to "shut your nose," as Carlito Morrell says, and you will have some idea of the physical comfort to be found in Havana. No wonder that Mrs. Cleveland is worn out after living 5 years in Such a Babel without one moment of quiet. O, I forgot the bells! the bells! They are never Still. Tinkle, tinkle, bang bang, squeak, squeak from morning till night and from night till morning, and at dawn a drum goes round to call the soldiers played by a man with no ear for music, which sets every nerve on edge. The Spaniards worship noise. It is the god of theirs Idolatry, together with dirt.

Our journey from Havana apart from the wracking over the horrid roads was beautiful. We passed magnificent estates among which the marquis of Thamos' was by no means the least superb. Oh such rows of palms! You have never conceived of any

thing so splendid as that tree and we passed rows that were miles
in length all alike, like a company of columns of white marble
with a corinthian capital of green. Mr [Burroughs], Carlos, a
confidential servant of Dr Morrell, and Andrès, who drove the
horses were our escort, and we were most carefully attended.
Mr B. and Carlos were on horseback, and we stopped at almost
every public place to get naranjada (orange water) & rest awhile,
and at the half way house I lay down. We arrived at Mrs Mor-
rells' at sun set, and Louisa received us very sweetly. I soon went
to bed as you may suppose & *slept soundly* all night! I sleep very
well and have a fine appetite, and have not had a touch of cold in
my head to which I am so subject at home. I ride on horseback
before breakfast, nay before sun rise, and then lie down two
hours, and as soon as the shadows grow long, ride again till dusk.
We breakfast at 1/2 past nine, and dine at 1/2 past three, and
take tea at 1/2 past eight. In the early morning coffee and
oranges are at our service & at breakfast there are eggs and meat,
plantains and coffee and milk, and coffee after dinner. My head
still aches a great deal, and I have not got over my weariness, but I

think both will yield in due time to such a climate. Every morning there is a golden sun rise, every evening a golden sunset. The stars are of every colour of the rainbow and this January moon is the brightest of the year. It is perfectly cool excepting at mid day and even then *I* am not too warm. I have on my merino dress now, which I have not taken off since I returned from my morning ride. Dr Morrell has taken my case in hand and determines to cure me. He is very interesting & Mrs Morrell is perfectly charming. The estates are beautiful I shall describe them in some future letter. San Juan is the name of the other. Edwardo is generally my cavalier and we ride to the most enchanting places; but never off Dr M's estates which are very large. I ride upon a serron, which is a pillow with a sort of basket upon it, easy as possible, my horse Rosillo is very good. We gathered beautiful flowers this morning, and broke our fast upon oranges, which we plucked from the tree with our own hands. I have no more time the mail goes. Love to Mary N. Thine ever, ever, dearest Mother & Father

Sophy.

Graham Greene

OUR MAN IN HAVANA

WORMOLD CAME AWAY from the Consulate Department carrying a cable in his breast-pocket. It had been shovelled rudely at him, and when he tried to speak he had been checked. "We don't want to know anything about it. A temporary arrangement. The sooner it's over the better we shall be pleased."

"Mr. Hawthorne said . . ."

"We don't know any Mr. Hawthorne. Please bear that in mind. Nobody of the name is employed here. Good morning."

Graham Greene drew on his experience as a secret service agent for his 1958 novel, Our Man in Havana. *Although Greene visited Cuba only briefly before writing the book, it accurately anticipates the Cuban Missile Crisis of 1962.*

He walked home. The long city lay spread along the open Atlantic; waves broke over the Avenida de Maceo and misted the windscreens of cars. The pink, grey, yellow pillars of what had once been the aristocratic quarter were eroded like rocks; an ancient coat of arms, smudged and featureless, was set over the doorway of a shabby hotel, and the shutters of a night-club were varnished in bright crude colours to protect them from the wet and salt of the sea. In the west the steel skyscrapers of the new town rose higher than lighthouses into the clear February sky. It was a city to visit, not a city to live in, but it was the city where Wormold had first fallen in love and he was held to it as though to the scene of a disaster. Time gives poetry to a battle-field, and perhaps Milly resembled a little the flower on an old rampart where an attack had been repulsed with heavy loss many years ago. Women passed him in the street marked on the fore-head with ashes as though they had come up into the sunlight from underground. He remembered that it was Ash Wednesday.

In spite of the school-holiday Milly was not at home when he reached the house—perhaps she was still at Mass or perhaps she was away riding at the Country Club. Lopez was demonstrating the Turbo Suction Cleaner to a priest's house-keeper who had rejected the Atomic Pile. Wormold's worst fears about the new model had been justified, for he had not suc-ceeded in selling a single specimen. He went upstairs and opened the telegram; it was addressed to a department in the British Consulate, and the figures which followed had an ugly look like the lottery tickets that remained unsold on the last day of a draw. There was 2674 and then a string of five-figure numerals: 42811 79145 72312 59200 80947 62533 10605 and so on. It was his first telegram and he noticed that it was addressed from Lon-don. He was not even certain (so long ago his lesson seemed) that he could decode it, but he recognized a single group, 59200, which had an abrupt and monitory appearance as though Hawthorne that moment had come accusingly up the stairs. Gloomily he took down Lamb's *Tales from Shakespeare*—how he had always detested Elia and the essay on Roast Pork. The first group of figures, he remembered, indicated the page, the line and the word with which the coding began. "Dionysia, the wicked wife of Cleon," he read, "met with an end proportionable to her deserts." He began to decode from "deserts." To his surprise something really did emerge. It was rather as though some strange inherited parrot had begun to speak. "No. I of 24 January following from 59200 begin paragraph A."

After working for three-quarters of an hour adding and subtracting, he had decoded the whole message apart from the final paragraph where something had gone wrong either with himself or 59200, or perhaps with Charles Lamb. "Following from 59200 begin paragraph A nearly a month since membership Country Club approved and no repeat no information concerning proposed sub-agents yet received stop trust you are not repeat not recruiting any sub-agents before having them properly traced stop begin paragraph B economic and political report on lines of questionnaire left with you should be despatched forthwith to 59200 stop begin paragraph C cursed galloon must be forwarded kingston primary tubercular message ends."

The last paragraph had an effect of angry incoherence which worried Wormold. For the first time it occurred to him that in their eyes—whoever *they* were—he had taken money and given nothing in return. This troubled him. It had seemed to him till then that he had been the recipient of an eccentric gift which had enabled Milly to ride at the Country Club and himself to order from England a few books he had coveted. The rest of the money was now on deposit in the bank; he half believed that some day he might be in a position to return it to Hawthorne.

He thought: I must do something, give them some names to trace, recruit an agent, keep them happy. He remembered how Milly used to play at shops and give him her pocket money for imaginary purchases. One had to play the child's game, but sooner or later Milly always required her money back.

He wondered how one recruited an agent. It was difficult for him to remember exactly how Hawthorne had recruited *him*—except that the whole affair had begun in a lavatory, but surely that was not an essential feature. He decided to begin with a reasonably easy case.

"You called me, Señor Vormell." For some reason the name Wormold was quite beyond Lopez' power of pronunciation, but as he seemed unable to settle on a satisfactory substitute, it was seldom that Wormold went by the same name twice.

"I want to talk to you, Lopez."

"*Si,* Señor Vomell."

Wormold said, "You've been with me a great many years now. We trust each other."

Lopez expressed the completeness of his trust with a gesture towards the heart.

"How would you like to earn a little more money each month?"

"Why, naturally . . . I was going to speak to you myself, Señor Ommel. I have a child coming. Perhaps twenty pesos?"

"This has nothing to do with the firm. Trade is too bad, Lopez. This will be confidential work, for me personally, you understand."

"Ah yes, Señor. Personal services I understand. You can trust me. I am discreet. Of course I will say nothing to the señorita."

"I think perhaps you *don't* understand."

"When a man reaches a certain age," Lopez said, "he no longer wishes to search for a woman himself, he wishes to rest from trouble. He wishes to command, 'Tonight yes, tomorrow night no.' To give his directions to someone he trusts . . ."

"I don't mean anything of the kind. What I was trying to say—well, it had nothing to do . . ."

"You do not need to be embarrassed in speaking to me, Señor Vormole. I have been with you many years."

"You are making a mistake," Wormold said. "I had no intention . . ."

"I understand that for an Englishman in your position places like the San Francisco are unsuitable. Even the Mamba Club."

Wormold knew that nothing he could say would check the eloquence of his assistant, now that he had embarked on the great Havana subject; the sexual exchange was not only the chief commerce of the city, but the whole *raison d'être* of a man's life. One sold sex or one bought it—immaterial which, but it was never given away.

"A youth needs variety," Lopez said, "but so too does a man of a certain age. For the youth it is the curiosity of ignorance, for the old it is the appetite which needs to be refreshed. No one can serve you better than I can, because I have studied you, Señor Venell. You are not a Cuban: for you the shape of a girl's bottom is less important than a certain gentleness of behaviour . . ."

"You have misunderstood me completely," Wormold said.

"The señorita this evening goes to a concert."

"How do you know?"

Lopez ignored the question. "While she is out, I will bring you a young lady to see. If you don't like her, I will bring another."

"You'll do nothing of the sort. Those are not the kind of services I want, Lopez. I want . . . well, I want you to keep your eyes and ears open and report to me . . ."

"On the señorita?"

"Good heavens no."

"Report on what then, Señor Vommold?"

Wormold said, "Well, things like . . ." But he hadn't

the faintest idea on what subjects Lopez was capable of reporting. He remembered only a few points in the long questionnaire and none of them seemed suitable, "Possible Communist infiltration of the armed forces; Actual figures of sugar- and tobacco-production last year." Of course there were the contents of waste-paper baskets in the offices where Lopez serviced the cleaners, but surely Hawthorne was joking when he spoke of the Dreyfus case, if those men ever joked.

"Like what, señor?"

Wormold said, "I'll let you know later. Go back to the shop now."

IT WAS THE hour of the daiquiri, and in the Wonder Bar Dr. Hasselbacher was happy with his second Scotch. "You are worrying still, Mr. Wormold?" he said.

"Yes, I am worrying."

"Still the cleaner—the Atomic cleaner?"

"Not the cleaner." He drained his daiquiri and ordered another.

"Today you are drinking very fast."

"Hasselbacher, you've never felt the need of money, have you? But then, you have no child."

"Before long you will have no child either."

"I suppose not." The comfort was as cold as the daiquiri. "When the time comes, Hasselbacher, I want us both to be away from here. I don't want Milly woken up by any Captain Segura."

"That I can understand."

"The other day I was offered money."

"Yes?"

"To get information."

"What sort of information?

"Secret information."

Dr. Hasselbacher sighed. He said, "You are a lucky man, Mr. Wormold. That information is always easy to give."

"Easy?"

"If it is secret enough, you alone know it. All you need is a little imagination, Mr. Wormold."

"They want me to recruit agents. How does one recruit an agent, Hasselbacher?"

"You could invent them too, Mr. Wormold."

"You sound as though you had experience."

"Medicine is my experience, Mr. Wormold. Have you never read the advertisement for secret remedies? A hair tonic confided by the dying Chief of a Red Indian tribe. With a secret remedy you don't have to print the formula. And there is something about a secret which makes people believe . . . perhaps a relic of magic. Have you read Sir James Frazer?"

"Have you heard of a book code?"

"Don't tell me too much, Mr. Wormold, all the same. Secrecy is not my business—I have no child. Please don't invent me as your agent."

"No, I can't do that. These people don't like our friendship, Hasselbacher. They want me to stay away from you. They are tracing you. How do you suppose they trace a man?"

"I don't know. Be careful, Mr. Wormold. Take their money, but don't give them anything in return. You are vulnerable to the Seguras. Just lie and keep your freedom. They don't deserve the truth."

"Whom do you mean by they?"

"Kingdoms, republics, powers." He drained his glass. "I must go and look at my culture, Mr. Wormold."

"Is anything happening yet?"

"Thank goodness, no. As long as nothing happens anything is possible, you agree? It is a pity that a lottery is ever drawn. I lose a hundred and forty thousand dollars a week, and I am a poor man."

"You won't forget Milly's birthday?"

"Perhaps the traces will be bad, and you will not want me to come. But remember, as long as you lie you do no harm."

"I take their money."

"They have no money except what they take from men like you and me."

He pushed open the half-door and was gone. Dr. Hasselbacher never talked in terms of morality; it was outside the province of a doctor.

Eduardo Galeano

CHRONICLE OF THE CITY OF HAVANA

HIS PARENTS HAD fled to the north. In those days, he and the revolution were both in their infancy. A quarter of a century later, Nelson Valdés traveled from Los Angeles to Havana to visit his homeland.

Every day at noon, Nelson would take the *guagua*, bus number 68, from the hotel entrance, to the José Martí Library. There he would read books on Cuba until nightfall.

One day at noon, *guagua* 68 screeched to a halt at an

Eduardo Galeano, born in Uruguay in 1940, is a journalist, historian, and political activist who was forced to flee his country in the 1970s; he was permitted to return in 1984. Galeano refers to his 1991 Book of Embraces as "little stories" that "reveal the great ones—the universe...through a keyhole."

intersection. There were cries of protest at the tremendous jolt until the passengers saw why the bus driver had jammed on the brakes: a magnificent woman had just crossed the street.

"You'll have to forgive me, gentlemen," said the driver of *guagua* 68, and he got out. All the passengers applauded and wished him luck.

The bus driver swaggered along, in no hurry, and the passengers watched him approach the saucy female, who stood on the corner, leaning against the wall, licking an ice cream cone. From *guagua* 68, the passengers followed the darting motion of her tongue as it kissed the ice cream while the driver talked on and on with no apparent result, until all at once she laughed and glanced up at him. The driver gave the thumbs-up sign and the passengers burst into a hearty ovation.

But when the driver went into the ice cream parlor, the passengers began to get restless. And when he came out a bit later with an ice cream cone in each hand, panic spread among the masses.

They beeped the horn. Someone leaned on it with all his might and honked like a burglar alarm, but the bus driver, deaf, nonchalant, was glued to the delectable woman.

Then, from the back of *guagua* 68, a woman with the appearance of a huge cannon ball, and an air of authority, stepped forward. Without a word, she sat in the driver's seat and put the engine in gear. *Guagua* 68 continued on its route, stopping at its customary stops, until the woman arrived at her own and got off. Another passenger took her place for a stretch, stopping at every bus stop, and then another, and another, and so *guagua* 68 continued on to the end of the line.

Nelson Valdés was the last one to get off. He had forgotten all about the library.

Henry Cabot Lodge

THE WAR WITH SPAIN

JUST AT THIS moment, when the unrighted wrong seemed about to force the inevitable decision, Mr. Cleveland went out of office, and with the interest awakened by a new administration, and the hopes of a changed policy, the immediate excitement subsided, and men who realized that however absorbing the tariff might be, the real and great question lay south of Florida, were content to wait and give to the new authority every possi-

In this excerpt from his memoirs, historian and statesman Henry Cabot Lodge tells of his and President McKinley's struggles with Cuba during the infamous war with Spain.

ble opportunity and assistance. The Republican party, which now returned to power, had taken a very strong ground at its convention in regard to Cuba, asserting practically that it would charge itself with the duty of compelling a final settlement of the question. President McKinley not only sympathized with the declaration of his party, but he felt profoundly the gravity of the Cuban situation, and cherished a deep desire to meet it successfully and conclusively. The question had been left in such an acute state, and so near to extreme action, by neglect of the cases of American prisoners, that it was plain that something must be done at once or the new administration would find itself plunged into hostilities before it had fairly taken the reins of power into its hands. The crucial point was the American prisoners, and President McKinley, less sensitive than his predecessor in regard to injuring the feelings of Spain, immediately demanded prompt release and redress in every case. His tone was so firm that the Spaniards at once gave way, and by the end of April every American prisoner had been released. With the removal of the immediate and crying evil the situation grew quieter, the crisis passed by, and the impending peril of war rolled back again into the distance. The cause of war would not come from Spanish outrages upon American citizens. So much was fixed by the President's decided action. But the question was still there, still moving and pressing, never at rest. And just when every one who was against doing anything was saying again contentedly that all was nicely over, and that the sham was a reality, and that there was no Cuban question, out the question would break in a new quarter. May 20, 1897, the Senate, without division, passed a joint resolution recognizing Cuban belligerency. This resolution, taking its usual course, had scarcely had time to reach the House and be sent by the Speaker to slumber in the Committee on Foreign Affairs, because there was not and ought not to be a Cuban question, when in came a message from the President on that very subject. It appeared oddly enough, that war was still going on, and that under the reconcentration system American citizens, as well as natives of the island, were being starved to death in Cuba. This the President, thoroughly informed by the consular reports, thought that he could not permit, and he therefore asked Congress for $50,000 to purchase and send supplies to these Americans who were being put to death by the methods of war employed by Spain. Congress gave the money at once, and the act was approved May 24, 1897. We demanded and received the assent of Spain, and thereupon ships were chartered and food sent to all the American consuls, in order to feed starving Americans. The Americans were fed, and many others not Americans also, and the United States by this action had at last interfered in Cuba; for no more complete act of intervention than this, which tended to cripple the military measures and check the starvation campaign of the Spaniards, could be imagined. It was not admitted, certainly not generally realized, that the United States had finally broken from the old policy of holding aloof, and had entered on the new policy of intervention in Cuba; but, nevertheless, the true answer to the unsettled question was beginning to draw visibly nearer.

Meantime the President, after careful consideration, selected General Stewart L. Woodford for minister to Spain—

the most important diplomatic post to be filled at this junc-
ture. No one could have been chosen who was more concilia-
tory than General Woodford, or more desirous to obtain a
peaceful solution of the ever-increasing differences with Spain.
With such a minister at Madrid it was certain that no effort
would be spared to soothe Spain and bring about an agreement calculated to gratify everybody, if such a thing were possible under the circumstances, which seemed unlikely, for it
looked as if the question had gone beyond the stage when it
could be dealt with by soft and gentle handling. Nevertheless,
until the new administration and the new President, through
the freshly appointed minister, could take up the thread of the
negotiations with Spain, there came a pause in the controversy
between the two nations. There was no pause in Cuba, no
pause in starving to death the miserable "reconcentrados," or
in the desolating raids of both combatants, which were fast
making the island a desert waste. There was no pause in the
agitation in the United States, or in the growth of the popular
feeling about Cuba and the horrid scenes there existent. The

unsettled question kept moving on, even though negotiations paused. Then came another delay, for before General Woodford reached Spain on September 1, Senor Canovas, the Prime Minister, was murdered, on Sunday, August 8, 1897, by an Italian anarchist. There was much alarm, a ministerial crisis, and then Senor Sagasta came in and formed a Liberal ministry. At last General Woodford was able to open his negotiations, and the demands of the United States were seriously pressed. We asked for the recall of Weyler, and, above all, for the revocation of the reconcentration edict. The new ministry made haste to comply in appearance with every request, and to promise everything we demanded. Then they asked in turn that we should give them opportunity to try autonomy in Cuba—another wrong answer to the old question, absolutely useless, and quite gone by in the autumn of 1897. But after all the ostensible compliance of the Sagasta ministry with our requests, the opportunity to try autonomy could not well be refused. The trouble was that, with the exception of the recall of Weyler, on October 9, 1897, about which no deception or postponement was possible, not one of these Spanish promises was worth the paper upon which it was written. It was all entirely characteristic of Spanish diplomacy, much vaunted by Spaniards, and much admired in Europe, and consisted simply of lying, evading, and making promises which there was no intention of performing. As the representatives of the United States tried to tell the truth, they laid themselves open to much European criticism for their rude diplomacy, and for not understanding the refined methods of older nations; but they had one grave disadvantage in a failure to realize that Spanish diplomacy consisted chiefly of falsehood, as it had done for some centuries, and that no faith could be put in anything they alleged or promised.

Meantime all agitation in the United States was restrained on the ground that after the Spanish concessions we were bound to give them a reasonable time to try autonomy, which was an entirely just view if the concessions had been real and autonomy either honest or practical. But as the weeks passed by it became apparent that autonomy was neither practical nor genuine; the atrocities and starvation went on despite the withdrawal of Weyler and the coming of the less brutal Blanco, and both Congress and people again began to grow restless.

The situation of the Americans in Havana also began to cause uneasiness, and there was so much disquiet that the administration very wisely determined to send a ship of war to that port. The battle-ship *Maine* was selected for this duty, and reached Havana on the morning of January 24, 1898. We were at peace with Spain, and we had an entire right to send a ship to any Cuban port. If it had been done, as it ought to have been done, at the beginning of the Cuban troubles, it would have excited no comment; but at this late date in the war it assumed an importance which did not rightfully belong to such an accident. The Spanish minister, Senor Dupuy de Lome, blustered in private and talked about war, but being informed quietly and decidedly by Mr. Day that the ship was going in any event, he quieted down in public, and the Spanish cruiser *Vizcaya* came to New York to demonstrate that the presence of the *Maine* at Havana was only a friendly visit. The sending of the *Maine* was received by the country with a sense of relief, and the action of the President was universally approved. Public attention, however, was soon distracted from this subject by an incident which in a flash revealed the utter worthlessness of all the Spanish concessions and promises. A letter of Senor Dupuy de Lome, dated December 25, 1897, and addressed to a friend, Senor Canalejas, had been stolen in Havana by some one in the Cuban interest, and sent to the Cuban Junta in New York, which gave it to the press on February 9, 1898. This letter contained a coarse and vulgar attack upon President McKinley, which led to the immediate resignation and recall of the writer, who had served Spain well and unscrupulously. But far more important in its wider bearings than this disclosure of the character of Dupuy de Lome was the fact that the letter revealed the utter hollowness of all the Spanish professions, and showed that the negotiations in regard to autonomy and commercial relations were only intended to amuse and deceive the United States. The effect of this revelation was just beginning to make itself felt when the American people were stunned by an event which drove everything else from their minds. On the morning of February 16 came the news that on the previous evening the battle-ship *Maine* had been blown up and totally destroyed in the harbor of Havana. The explosion occurred under the forward part of the ship, and 264 men and two officers were killed. The overt act had come. This gigantic murder of sleeping men in the fancied security of a friendly harbor was the direct outcome and the perfect expression of Spanish rule, the appropriate action of a corrupt system struggling in its last agony. At last in very truth the unsettled question had come home to the United States, and it spoke this time in awful tones, which rang loud and could not be silenced. A wave of fierce wrath swept over the American people. But a word was needed, and war would have come then in response to this foul and treacherous act of war, for such in truth it was. But the words of Captain Sigsbee, the commander of the *Maine,* whose coolness, self-restraint, and high courage were beyond praise, asking, even in the midst of the slaughter, that judgment should be suspended, were heeded alike by government and people.

Scarcely a word was said in either House or Senate, and for forty days the American people and the American Congress waited in silence for the verdict of the board of naval officers who had been appointed to report on the destruction of the *Maine.* To those who understood the American people this grim silence, this stern self-control, were more threatening than any words of sorrow or of anger could possibly have been. Spain, rushing ignorantly, arrogantly, on her doom, understood nothing. A generous sympathy, a prompt offer to make every reparation, while she disclaimed all guilt, and she could have turned the current of feeling and gone far to save herself and her colonies. Instead of that, with incredible stupidity and utter meanness of soul, she announced, before any one had even looked at the wreck, that the ship was blown up from the inside, owing to the carelessness of the American officers. Her ambassadors abroad reiterated this ministerial falsehood, and, not content with that, insulted the brave men who had the *Maine* in charge, while official Spaniards everywhere insinuated or declared that lack of discipline was what blew up the battle-ship. There was much anger, mostly of the very silent sort, in the United States as these charges flew on wires and cables about the world; but the American reply to them was not given until some months later on May 1 and July 3 when certain proofs were given of the discipline and quality of American sailors which even Spain could not overlook. Still the Spanish attitude in regard to the *Maine* had one undoubted merit—it moved the unsettled question forward, and made a wrong answer more difficult than ever.

Ernest Hemingway

MARLIN OFF THE MORRO

THE ROOMS ON the northeastern corner of the Ambos Mundos Hotel in Havana look out, to the north, over the old cathedral, the entrance to the harbor, and the sea, and to the east to Casablanca peninsula, the roofs of all houses in between and the width of the harbor. If you sleep with your feet toward the east, this may be against the tenets of certain religions, the sun, coming up over the Casablanca side and into

Sports aficionado Ernest Hemingway (1899–1961) discovered marlin fishing, which he called "completely and utterly satisfying as a sport, a living, a spectacle, and a form of exercise," in Cuba in 1932. In 1940 he purchased a house outside Havana, Finca Vigía, which he owned and lived in periodically for the rest of his life. The year before his death he declared himself to be a "true Cuban."

your open window, will shine on your face and wake you no matter where you were the night before. If you do not choose to get up you can turn around the other way in the bed or roll over. That will not help for long because the sun will be getting stronger and the only thing to do is close the shutter.

Getting up to close the shutter you look across the harbor to the flag on the fortress and see it is straightened out toward you. You look out the north window past the Morro and see that the smooth morning sheen is rippling over and you know the trade wind is coming up early. You take a shower, pull on an old pair of khaki pants and a shirt, take the pair of moccasins that are dry, put the other pair in the window so they will be dry next night, walk to the elevator, ride down, get a paper at the desk, walk across the corner to the cafe and have breakfast.

There are two opposing schools about breakfast. If you knew you were not going to be into fish for two or three hours, a good big breakfast would be the thing. Maybe it is a good thing anyway but I do not want to trust it, so drink a glass of vichy, a glass of cold milk and eat a piece of Cuban bread, read the papers and walk down to the boat. I have hooked them on a full stomach in that sun and I do not want to hook any more of them that way.

We have an ice-box that runs across the stern of the boat with bait iced down on one side and beer and fruit iced on the other. The best bait for big marlin is fresh cero mackerel or kingfish of a pound to three pounds weight. The best beer is Hatuey, the best fruits, in season, are Filipino mangoes, iced pineapple, and alligator pears. Ordinarily we eat the alligator pears for lunch with a sandwich, fixing them with pepper and salt and a freshly squeezed lime. When we run into the beach to anchor, swim and cook a hot lunch on days, when fish are not running you can make a French dressing for the pears, adding a little mustard. You can get enough fine, big avocados to feed five people for fifteen cents.

The boat is the Anita, thirty-four feet long, very able in a sea, with plenty of speed for these fish, owned and skippered by Capt. Joe Russell of Key West who brought the first load of liquor that ever came into that place from Cuba and who knows more about swordfish than most Keywesters do about grunts. The other man on board is the best marlin and swordfisherman around Cuba, Carlos Gutierrez, of Zapata, 31, Havana, 54 years old, who goes Captain on a fishing smack in the winter and fishes marlin commercially in the summer. I met him six years ago in Dry Tortugas and first heard about the big marlin that run off Cuba from him. He can, literally, gaff a dolphin through the head back-handed and he has studied the habits of the marlin since he first went fishing for them as a boy of twelve with his father.

As the boat leaves the San Francisco wharf, tarpon are rolling in the slip. Going out of the harbor you see more of them rolling near the live fish cars that are buoyed alongside the line of anchored fishing smacks. Off the Morro in the entrance to the harbor there is a good coral bottom with about twenty fathoms of water and you pass many small boats bottom fishing for mutton fish and red snappers and jigging for mackerel and occasional kingfish. Outside the breeze freshens and as far as you can see the small boats of the marlin fishermen are scattered. They are fishing with four to six heavy handlines in from forty to seventy fathoms drifting for the fish that are travelling deep. We troll for the ones that are on the surface feeding, or travelling, or cruising fifteen or twenty fathoms down. They see the two big teasers or the baits and come up with a smash, usually going head and shoulders out of the water on the strike.

Marlin travel from east to west against the current of the gulf stream. No one has ever seen them working in the other direction, although the current of the gulf stream is not so stable; sometimes, just before the new moon, being quite slack and at others running strongly to the westward. But the prevailing wind is the northeast trade and when this blows the marlin come to the top and cruise with the wind, the scythe tail, a light, steely lavender, cutting the swells as it projects and goes under; the big fish, yellow looking in the water, swimming two or three feet under the surface, the huge pectoral fins tucked close to the flanks, the dorsal fin down, the fish looking a round, fast-moving log in the water except for the erect curve of that slicing tail.

The heavier the current runs to the eastward the more marlin there are; travelling along the edge of the dark, swirling current from a quarter of a mile to four miles off shore; all going in the same direction like cars along a highway. We have been fighting a fish, on days when they were running well, and see six others pass close to the boat during a space of half an hour.

As an indication of how plentiful they are, the official report from the Havana markets from the middle of March to the 18th of July this year showed eleven thousand small marlin and one hundred and fifty large marlin were brought into the market by the commercial fishermen of Santa Cruz del Norte, Jaruco, Guanabo, Cojimar, Havana, Chorrera, Marianao, Jaimanitas, Baracoa, Banes, Mariel and Cabañas. Marlin are caught at Matanzas and Cardenas to the east and at Bahía Honda to the west of the towns mentioned but those fish are not shipped to Havana. The big fish had only been running two weeks when this report was compiled.

Fishing with rod and reel from the middle of April through the 18th of July of this season we caught fifty-two marlin and two sailfish. The largest black marlin was 468 pounds, and 12 feet 8 inches long. The largest striped marlin was 343 pounds and 10 feet five inches. The biggest white marlin weighed 87 pounds and was 7 feet 8 inches in length.

The white marlin runs first in April and May, then come the immature striped marlin with brilliant stripes which fade after the fish dies. These are most plentiful in May and run into June. Then come the black and striped marlin together. The biggest run of striped marlin is in July and as they get scarce the very big black marlin come through until into September and later. Just before the striped marlin are due to run the smaller marlin drop off altogether and it seems, except for an occasional school of small tuna and bonito, as though the gulf stream were empty. There are so many color variations, some of them caused by feed, others by age, others by the depth of water, in these marlin that anyone seeking notoriety for himself by naming new species could have a field day along the north Cuba coast. For me they are all color and sexual variations of the same fish. This is too complicated a theory to go into a letter.

The marlin hit a trolled bait in four different ways. First, with hunger, again with anger, then simply playfully, last with indifference. Anyone can hook a hungry fish who gives him enough line, doesn't backlash and sets the hook hard enough. What happens then is something else. The main thing is to loosen your drag quickly enough when he starts to jump and make his run, and get the boat after him as he heads out to sea. The hungry marlin smashes at the bait with bill, shoulders, top fin and tail out. If he gets one bait he will turn and charge the other. If you pull the bait out of his mouth he will come for it again as long as there is any bait on the hook.

The angry fish puzzled us for a long time. He would come from below and hit the bait with a smash like a bomb exploding in the water. But as you slacked line to him he has dropped it. Screw down on the drag and race the bait in and he would slam it again without taking it. There is no way to hook a fish acting that way except to strike hard as he smashes. Put the drag on, speed up the boat and sock him as he crashes it. He slams the bait to kill it as long as it seems to be alive.

The playful marlin, probably one who has fed well, will come behind a bait with his fin high, shove his bill clear out of water and take the bait lightly between his bill and pointed lower jaw. When you turn it loose to him he drops it. I am speaking of absolutely fresh bait caught that same day; if the bait were stale you might expect them all to refuse it once they had tasted it. This sort of fish can often be made to hit by speeding the boat up and skipping the bait over the top of the water with the rod. If he does take it, do not give him too much line before you hit him.

The indifferent fish will follow the boat for as many as three or four miles. Looking the baits over, sheering away, coming back to swim deep down below them and follow, indifferent to the bait, yet curious. If such a fish swims with his pectoral fins tucked close to his sides he will not bite. He is cruising and you are on his course. That is all. The minute a marlin sees the bait, if he is going to strike, he raises his dorsal fin and spreads those wide, bright blue pectorals so that he looks like some great, under-sea bird in the water as he follows.

The black marlin is a stupid fish. He is immensely powerful, can jump wonderfully and will break your back sounding but he has not the stamina of the striped marlin, nor his intelligence. I believe they are mostly old, female fish, past their prime and that it is age that gives them that black color. When they are younger they are much bluer and the meat, too, is whiter. If you fight them fast, never letting up, never resting, you can kill them quicker than you could ever kill a striped marlin of the same size. Their great strength makes them very dangerous for the first forty minutes. I mean dangerous to the tackle; no fish is dangerous to a man in a launch. But if you can take what they have to give during that time and keep working on them they will tire much quicker than any striped marlin. The 468 pounder was hooked in the roof of the mouth, was in no way tangled in the leader, jumped eight times completely clear, towed the boat stern first when held tight, sounded four times, but was brought to gaff at the top of the water, fin and tail out, in sixty-five minutes. But if I had not lost a much larger striped marlin the day before after two hours and twenty minutes, and fought a black one the day before for forty-five I would not have been in shape to work him so hard.

Fishing in a five-mile-an-hour current, where a hooked fish will always swim against the current, where the water is from four hundred to seven hundred fathoms deep, there is much to learn about tactics in fighting big fish. But one myth that can be dissipated is the old one that the water pressure at one thousand feet will kill the fish. A marlin dies at the bottom only if he has been hooked in the belly. These fish are used to going to the bottom. They often feed there. They are not built like bottom fish which live always at the same depth but are built to be able to go up and down in any depth. I have had a marlin sound four hundred yards straight down, all the rod under water over the side, bent double with that weight going down, down, down, watching the line go, putting on all pressure possible on the reel to check him, him going down and down until you are sure every inch of line will go. Suddenly he stops sounding and you straighten up, get onto your feet, get the butt in the socket and work him up slowly, finally you have the double line on the reel and think he is coming to gaff and then the line begins to rip out as he hooks up and heads off to sea just under the surface to come out in ten long, clean jumps. This after an hour and a half of fight. Then to sound again. They are a fish all right. The 343 pounder jumped 44 times.

You can fish for them in Cuba from April all through the summer. Big ones will be accidental until the middle of June and we only saw four broadbill all season. But in July and August it is even money any day you go out that you will hook into a fish from three hundred pounds up. Up means a very long way up. The biggest marlin ever brought into the market by the commercial fishermen weighed eleven hundred and seventy-five pounds with head cut off, gutted, tail cut off and flanks cut away; eleven hundred and seventy-five pounds when on the slab, nothing but the saleable meat ready to be cut into steaks. All right. You tell me. What did he weigh in the water and what did he look like when he jumped?

James Steele

CUBAN SKETCHES

THE FIRST GLIMPSE of the island was a contradiction of all I expected to see; a couple of knobs of land, as bald as a monk's pate each one, called the "Pan of the Matanzas," because the twin hills are imagined to resemble in shape those little brown, crusty, cold biscuits they know as bread in Cuba. By the time, however, you have duly enquired about them of the captain, as it is every passenger's duty to do, you are very near "the finest harbor in the world," and find various other

As he himself put it, James William Steele "did not visit the country for the purpose of describing it, wished himself somewhere else while there, and while he stayed was chiefly occupied in collecting... the princely income of an United States Consul." Cuban Sketches was published in 1881.

things to call away your attention. No one entering the narrow strait of green water into the harbor of Havana for the first time, realizes the striking peculiarity of the situation that occurs to him very prominently afterward. You are only ninety miles from the winking light-houses and sandy shore of Florida, but you have entered dominions as foreign, as different, as full of strangeness, as though you had sailed around the world to find them.

A low-lying city of parti-colored architecture, whose walls are red, blue, green, and yellow, lies before you; a city in which there is not a chimney, a cooking-stove, a hotel-elevator, a four-story house, or a sidewalk three feet wide, and yet a city of near three hundred thousand souls. I may as well proceed from this, and remark also that there are no glass windows, and not a night-latch in the place, nor a hair mattress or a carpeted room. When, after a bustle and strife and competitive swearing unparalleled, you get your baggage down over the side by a line, and yourself and your belongings ashore in a crazy and comfortless boat, you wonder when you are to emerge from the maze of what you take to be alleys and by-ways and enter the open street. But you finally discover that these alleys and by-ways *are* the streets, and deemed magnificent avenues.

As YOU WANDER around with a feeling creeping over you that you wish you had not come, you encounter odd bits of ancient and battered wall, with the remains of bartizan and parapet still visible in decay, overgrown with ivy and ferns. A long time ago, these were the defense and pride of the walled city of Havana. There is a huge and dismantled church now used as a custom-house store-room, but in its day a pretentious structure, desecrated and rendered unfit for holy uses by having been used as a stable by the irreverent English during their occupation of the place. There is another church, where you may see a small, square stone tablet in the wall, behind which are said to lie the bones of Columbus. There is an unsatisfactory uncertainty about it now, as well as a church quarrel, for they have found the tomb and coffin of the renowned explorer in another church, upon the island where he died and was buried. However, it is of no consequence. He was the man, wherever he lies, who, with the genius and daring to cross an unknown sea and discover a world, with a crew of sailors who believed they were constantly in danger of getting too near the edge and sliding off, yet died without knowing what he had discovered, or even that Cuba was an island. Cervantes and Columbus are the two great men of Spain. There is a statue of one or the other, or both, in every plaza on the island. Yet one of them was not a Spaniard, and the final resting-place of the renowned author of "Don Quixote" no man knoweth.

It is impossible to avoid the impression, during the first few days, that the weather will surely change. Perhaps you left the snow falling beautifully in the North, and a nor'easter howling, and it is difficult to realize that any thing so cutting and powerful can have no effect except within limits that seem disproportionately small. There is something new, and not agreeable, in your sense of the untimely heat, and the air that never felt the purifying touch of frost seems to you not quite fit for human breathing. The smells assail you, and, while they are not of Araby, yet seem to have no definite place in any catalogue known to you. In the huge and bare apartment in the hotel in which you are to begin to learn to sleep in a Cuban bed, you gaze despairingly into trunks that contain nothing you can wear. Your boots hurt you, and seem to make a noise like the tramp of a troop of cavalry over a bridge as you pace the tiled floors. In your total unlikeness and inability to all your surroundings, it requires some degree of self-respect not to begin to regard yourself as a monstrosity. You have the idea that the natives are thinking you a fair specimen from the barbarous hordes of the Arctic Circle. The cries of the street fall upon your ear, and cause within you a disagreeable apprehension that some one is being murdered. But it is only one who sells eggs.

In the morning the breakfast hour eludes you, not because it is too early, but because it is too late. Ere it comes you feel that you are likely to starve. This is at first. Afterward it becomes, like all other breakfasts with reference to your habits, quite early enough. When at last the hour arrives, very nearly a New York lunch-time, there is nothing to eat that ever you ate before. The cut-glass before you contains oil, and the first dish you taste, and every one that comes after, has been cooked in the same. There is also, perchance, a spice of the delightful vegetable that, as is said, every thing Spanish smells of. There is no butter, and will never be; no fresh bread, and none of any kind that can be bitten or broken. There is no use in trying to change any of these things, for it is not a country favorable to reforms. "Pies an' cakes," and the long array of things that suffer under the easy and general accusation of being "indigestible" in the United States, and are long since incorporated in the phraseology of your country, are here unknown. A few years' residence in Cuba will give you "a realizing sense" of how good they are. But, meantime, you may partially comfort yourself with the idea that people are quite as bilious here as elsewhere, notwithstanding the deprivation.

One essential item of daily comfort and necessity will call for the pilgrim's serious attention ere he is safely through the first twenty-four hours,—the bed he is to sleep in. There are those who like it, but I regard it, and have always, as too thin. It is merely a sheet of linen stretched as tight as a drum-head between four posts. A couple of sheets and a very undowny pillow complete the luxurious couch. But the bed is nothing, as you learn after a while,—nothing comparatively. It is the mosquito net that is essential. When, in the stillness of the night you hear the hum of the gathering hosts, you are disposed to be quite content with any thing that is inside the net. If you are inclined to entomology, you may easily learn that this is no ordinary mosquito, and that, besides other interesting characteristics, he has stripes upon his legs that you can count.

There are parks in Havana. They mention them often, and speak of them with pride. There are in these, statues of Columbus and Cervantes, some artful little trees, a fountain or two, and some dusty walks. They are the barest and dustiest efforts after pleasure-grounds ever made. There are hardly ten yards of shade, unless it be the shadow of a building, and there is no green grass or any thing that looks or feels cool. It is an interesting fact that the Spaniard hates trees, and after an indiscriminate slaughter of them in all regions he has ever occupied, they decline to grow for him when he plants them in a park. Yet, it is a climate that has hardly a vicissitude. The whole year is summer-time, and the soil is rich beyond any other. I do not know why the places of resort in a land where life might be passed out of doors, should depend for their attractiveness upon gas-light and a crowd. The queen of the tropics is essentially a sad and lonesome city, though as rich, as frivolous, and as wicked, as was Pompeii.

There are essentials in which all the cities of Cuba are alike. There are other respects in which the city of Havana is unique. Representatives of every race and clime may be found there, and the flags of every nation float in her harbor. The streets are as busy as Babel, and business has been found so remunerative that her citizens are the most extravagant, as a class, in the world. But nothing has changed in the least degree the ancient Spanish character; nothing ever will. Individuality is the strong characteristic of the Latin, the Chinaman, and the American Indian.

The bay of Havana almost is, as they are fond of saying, the finest in the world. It lies in the figure of a man's hand, the opening at the wrist, and the fingers extending in all directions. The anchorage is good, and the water deep and nasty. A canal was begun a long time ago that, when finished, will allow a current to pass through the bay, and mitigate or banish the perpetual scourge of yellow fever. But it was never finished, and will never be. In all the magnificent haven there is not a landing-pier, quay, or dock, or a decent landing. All vessels, except small schooners under the Spanish flag, load and unload in the stream. It is not deemed prudent to permit foreign vessels to come too near. No one but a Spaniard may engage in the occupation of lightering, or loading and unloading vessels, and if there were quays, this occupation and its attendant fees would be lost. The government stands in this representative foreign capital in the position of "hands off," and warns all mankind that she does not propose to take any risks of foreign contamination.

Sunset is the hour for closing business at Moro Castle, and no matter what storms may be brooding outside, no vessel may come in until the following day. This is an ancient regulation of the place, without regard to the fact that a harbor is, in a certain sense, the property of the world, not to be closed like a shop when the owner retires. Parallel with this is the fact that, after nigh three hundred years' possession, the Spanish government does not own a custom-house building on the island, or any others, save the "palaces" and jails, and a dilapidated barracks, and a hospital or two. Moro Castle carries the only light-house, so far as I ever heard, upon a coast indented with innumerable bays and lined with shoals. The old times, the ancient slowness, the time-honored inefficiency, are visible everywhere. Sick soldiers beg in the streets. Ragged battalions of boy recruits come over from Spain, hatless, shoeless, and destitute. And yet, military display is a passion, and the Cubans pay twenty-four millions a year for the support of an army to keep them on the under side.

But everybody enjoys himself in Havana. Laziness is natural, universal, and reputable. The avoidance of heat, worry, work, and perspiration, and good judgment as to the shadiest side of every way of life, are the essentials of tropical happiness. Clothing is airy, and the body at ease, through the absence of the bundlings and wraps necessary where the snow flies. The necessity for manual labor is a disgrace and misfortune combined. *Los negros* were designed for that, and the white is expected to see it done, and be the beneficiary. There is no other city that has so many youth engaged exclusively in smoking paper cigars and fondling canes, to whom life is a dream, and personal adornment the sole ambition. Foppery is so common that it does not exist, indolence so natural that it excites no remark, and ambition and endeavor are follies.

How tiresome it grows! These are not those of whom the kings of men will ever come. It is a people of smiles, glances, easy talk, time-killing, dilettante. Except those who are obliged to work, and they are beneath consideration.

Margarita Engle

SINGING TO CUBA

"YOU LOOK MORE Cuban than Yanqui," said the cab-driver as he turned to inspect me. I wished I had found a taxi farther away from the hotel. This driver seemed too interested in my activities. I had been warned that taxi drivers were often members of the Communist Party, men whose careers advanced by turning people in to the secret police for any suspicious movements or statements. I didn't want to keep lying but I had entered Cuba disguised as a

---

Margarita Engle is a botanist and writer born in Los Angeles to an American father and Cuban mother. After decades of unsuccessful applications for permission to go to the island, she visited her mother's family in 1991 and 1992. Singing to Cuba is her fictionalized account of that visit.

tourist, and now I would have to continue pretending.

I laughed and said, "Really?" treating his comment as a joke. As we arrived at Miguelito's familiar house, I looked up at the crumbling stone and peeling white paint faded to gray. I looked across at the park with its big trees and at the sea beyond, the harbor nearly inactive now that Soviet and East German ships were no longer arriving. I felt like a person in a dream, seeing things remembered from some other era of existence, wondering which was real, the dream or the memory.

I paid the driver and told him not to wait, I would be visiting for at least an hour. He left with a friendly wave and I decided perhaps my sense of being followed and watched was paranoia from seeing too many spy movies about communist countries. But uncle Juan had told me not to trust anybody in Cuba, not even family, and my grandmother Amparo had told me she was afraid I could be arrested the minute I stepped off the plane just because I was a relative of Gabriel's.

I walked up a series of old marble steps to Miguelito's heavy wooden door. Nothing had changed. The house was still here, although peeling and crumbling. The park was still green and graceful, the sea still sparkling, the sky still blue streaked with black storm clouds. The air was hot and moist, scented by *alelí* and Madagascar jasmine. I hesitated at the door, suddenly feeling ridiculous showing up after so many years to meet a cousin I hadn't seen since he was four, intending to tell him he wasn't forgotten. Why should he believe me and, what's more, why should he care? In the U.S., such a visit would be unimaginable.

I knocked and waited, my anticipation slipping away as the wooden door remained shut. Relief and disappointment combined as I decided that my cousin was probably away on vacation or at work, or perhaps he had moved without informing relatives in the U.S.

I knocked again just to be sure and waited again. I was just about to turn away, telling myself at least I had tried, when the door creaked slightly open and a face peered out. A tall, slender man looked down at me. He was handsome, with a full dark moustache that gave him the appearance of a cowboy in a movie about the American West. He looked like he should be wearing chaps and spurs.

He leaned down toward me, and for a few seconds we were both silent as I tried to figure out how to introduce myself. His serious expression suddenly gave way to a youthful smile, and he reached out from behind the door to embrace me with one arm.

"I know who you are!" he said softly, shaking an index finger the way people do when they say, "Aha!"

Delighted that he could recognize me after thirty-one years, I laughed, and followed him as he led me behind the wooden door and up another marble staircase inside the house.

"They divided the house and gave the rest to other families," he explained as we climbed. The house, by North American standards, would not be considered large, but it had once been very elegant, one of the homes built to house colonial Spanish gentry long before the island gained its independence.

We reached the top story, and I realized that this house which, in the old Cuba, might have harbored many branches of the same family, now held several unrelated families, like apartment buildings in the U.S.

Miguelito ushered me into a familiar many-windowed room wrapped in sunlight and furnished with hand-carved mahogany from the precious-wood forests which had once covered the island. My cousin led me to a big rocking chair in front of a window which faced the park. He sat me down in front of a portrait of my great-grandmother, my grandmother Amparo's mother, the mother of my great uncle Gabriel and of Miguelito's own father, Miguel. The portrait looked out across the park as if the old woman's image could enjoy looking at swaying trees and the sea beyond. In front of the portrait stood a small altar with flowers, candles and an image of Cuba's patron Saint, *La Virgen de la Caridad del Cobre,* Our Lady of Charity of Cobre.

I sat alone with the memory of my great-grandmother while Miguelito vanished down a dark hallway. This interval gave me a chance to enjoy my journey into the past, my sense of encountering the familiar unharmed—the park, the sea, the house, the portrait, my cousin.

Miguelito returned leading his mother. She was now stooped and very old. She was one of the thinnest women I had ever seen, so frail it seemed a careless touch could shatter her into countless pieces of fine crystal. I remembered her as a beautiful woman, gracious, the descendant of wealthy Spaniards, a woman who had stepped into an unfamiliar realm when she married my great-uncle Miguel, the son of rugged *guajiros,* still chopping their own cane and milking their own cows on a remote sweep of green hills far away from the elegance of Havana.

Miguelito's mother walked holding onto her son with one hand and to the peeling wall with the other.

"My mother," said Miguelito. "She's afraid of walking, afraid she'll fall." He had noticed that I was wondering why she held onto the wall. "The government," he then added, "does not believe in paint." Again he had read my thoughts.

"The whole city is falling down," he said. "Everything is peeling and crumbling: the paint, the stone, the statues. Houses are collapsing while people still live in them. But what can you do? You can't move. No one moves in

Cuba, unless they can find someone who wants to trade houses. We're not allowed to sell our house or buy a new one, and there's no paint or plaster or any kind of materials to fix anything."

He led his mother to another rocking chair facing mine. Then he found one for himself and, looking around the room, I realized that rocking chairs were the only seats available. They were scattered all over the room, big, imposing rocking chairs. As a child I had always loved hammocks and rocking chairs. I had associated them with stability, with relaxation, patience, a dreamy state of mind found only in the very young and very old.

Miguelito turned to his mother and explained, "This is Amparo's granddaughter. She came from over there to see us." The old woman studied me, her memory struggling. "Aah," she finally sighed. "From the other side." She smiled at me, and added, "People used to do that, you know, go to the other side for awhile and come back. Now they never come back."

Understanding that she meant exiled family members never returned to Cuba anymore, I nodded and said, "Perhaps someday they will again." I offered her a piece of strawberry candy wrapped in red foil with the ends twisted like Chinese fans. She took it and held it until her son explained what it was, unwrapping the candy for her and showing her that the foil could be discarded.

"Aah," she repeated, "*caramelitos,* I remember them."

Miguelito tilted his head slightly in a gesture that indicated patience, and told me, "Things like this, candies, small things, here they don't exist anymore."

I smiled in sympathy. "Nothing inside this room has changed," I said, "the view, the way the sun comes in these windows." I found the view exhilarating, the room light and airy, the company of people I hadn't seen for so long enchanting. I felt like a child again, fascinated by every detail of my surroundings.

Miguelito stood abruptly and flung the windows wide open, one at a time, in a ceremonial manner. Still facing the windows, he stood absorbing the sea breeze and announced in a loud voice, "This is my house, and I will say whatever I want to say. I don't care if they take me away to the prison camps, because what do I have left to lose?"

He turned to face me. He seemed very tall and dignified, proud. "What do I have left to lose?" he asked, and suddenly his shoulders slumped and he moved away from the window. Seated once again, he leaned close to me and said, "Look, you came out of an airplane, right? But you might as well have come out of a spaceship, walking upside down." He used the fingers of one hand to illustrate how space creatures might walk, legs pointed up instead of down.

His gaze searched my face for understanding. I nodded. "That," he said, "is how different your life has been from mine."

For a moment I was afraid he was angry with me, but soon he smiled and I saw that his bitterness was not against those who had escaped to outer space.

"We have a son," he said cheerfully. Then he left me with his mother and, disappearing down the dark hallway, he went to fetch his wife and child. I sat alone with the old woman, saying nothing, the two of us rocking and looking out the window, remembering.

When Miguelito returned with his wife, she embraced me and introduced their child who, like my cousin and my great-uncle Miguel, was already very tall.

"Do you know how we recognized you?" my cousin's wife asked, grinning. She was very beautiful and wonderfully warm. I felt myself enveloped by peace, the hot fragrant air, the breeze coming in through the open windows, the return to a reality I had feared might no longer exist, the recognition.

"Aurora," Miguelito urged, "show her the picture." His wife left to find a box of photographs, and she came back holding one that Amparo had sent of my wedding day, a younger version of myself smiling and holding a bouquet of orange blossoms and roses, my North American husband smiling at my side.

"What I remember about you," Miguelito said, shaking a finger as if to scold me, "is the way you liked to play with spiders and lizards." He grimaced and shuddered in an exaggerated manner, just as he had when he was little. "You caught those huge terrible spiders," he said, revealing that he was a true city dweller, still afraid of tarantulas. "And you would carry them around in your hand!"

His wife also made a face indicating disgust.

"I still prefer the countryside," I laughed, explaining that in some ways I hadn't changed much.

"*¡Qué horror!*" Miguelito responded, still picturing me playing with tarantulas, not realizing that to me the real horrors were in the city: gray sky, the odor of fumes, mile after mile of paved streets with no trees to dance when a breeze came along, and the junkies, pimps and gangs, and the curling smoke of my opium, laced with dreams of dragons and mermaids, gargoyles and sirens.

Yet I understood my cousin's childhood fear of spiders because I had also been frightened by a beast in Cuba. It happened before Miguelito's birth, when I was only two, and we were on the island visiting my grandmother and all her family in Havana and Trinidad.

It was the summer of 1953, when Fidel Castro had launched his first attack against the forces of Batista. The attack failed and Castro was arrested, but later he was released and went into exile in Mexico, returning on a small boat with a band of *guerrilla* warriors who landed near the eastern mountains of Oriente province. This time they fought until they succeeded in deposing the tyrant hated by peasants like Gabriel.

The beast which terrified me while Fidel was attacking Moncada was an enormous anaconda at the Havana Zoo. I was walking hand in hand with my *Abuelita* Amparo, and beside her were her brothers Miguel and Daniel. Gabriel was on his farm, and Isabelita was in Trinidad painting rural Cuban landscapes and portraits of my great-grandmother.

When we passed the anaconda's cage the adults were talking and laughing. No one else seemed to notice the great serpent's hunger. I stopped, and met the snake's greedy stare, certain that the beast intended to consume me. Too young to speak or think, I stood transfixed by terror. That moment became frozen in time and was lost deep within my memory until many years later when it emerged, along with other trapped memories and visions of demons.

Now, facing Miguelito as he reminded me how frightened he had been when he saw me exploring Cuba's soil for small wild creatures, I wondered whether, during all the years of separation, he had thought of me only when he thought of gruesome beasts.

I pulled out a bag filled with candy, each wrapper decorated with the image of some colorful northern fruit, strawberries, apples, peaches. Miguelito, Aurora and the old woman all stared hard at the mound of candies, at the fishtails of twisted foil, the inside of each wrapper silvery like fish scales. I poured the candies out of the bag onto a dish Miguelito held out to catch them. He and his wife exchanged glances, shaking their heads as if they had seen something wondrous.

They passed the dish of candy around, admiring the colors and gleam. Aurora said she wanted to show them to her friends. Only the old lady tasted the sweets. I brought out all the other gifts sent by exiled relatives, the soaps, T-shirts, diapers, baseball caps, spools of thread, safety pins, flashlights, calculators, canned sausage, coffee, chewing gum.

Miguelito sniffed at a package of gum. "It's been a long time," he said softly. Aurora smelled the soaps, and said, "It's these little things we forget here, smells, tastes, designs, details." Little, I thought, but perhaps not insignificant.

"And choices," my cousin added. "Sometimes I think what would it be like to have a choice. Tell me, for instance, is it true your husband can walk into a big store full of beer and choose from several different kinds, any kind he wants, and each one will taste different?"

I nodded. "Dozens of kinds. Maybe hundreds."

"And which does he like best?" Miguelito asked, looking like a child caught up in a fantasy world, imagining something too beautiful to be true, a world of unicorns and dragons, leprechauns and wishes granted by magic.

I tried to remember which brands my husband asked for when I went grocery shopping. "Coors," I said, "or Millers and imported kinds too, I guess, Corona." I remembered all the brands he'd tried on occasion, names like Moosehead, or beers from exotic places like Singapore and Ceylon, with decorative labels that looked like pages out of a National Geographic magazine.

"Here," my cousin told me, "we have one kind of beer only. It comes in a brown bottle with no label, government beer, produced by the State. I would be curious to taste different flavors. This year," he continued, "there is plenty of beer and ice cream but little else. They give us beer to make up for all the food shortages, and to try to make up for canceling carnival on account of the economic crisis."

In Cuba, there had once been many saints' day carnivals, as well as the one before Lent. Now the main carnival was supposed to commemorate Revolution Day, July 26, the anniversary of Fidel's attack on the Moncada Barracks during the summer of 1953.

I looked out at the hot sky with its black clouds.

"It is very unlikely," my cousin said wistfully, "that they would ever let me travel." I knew he meant the government when he said "they." In New York, Amparo and Juan always said "they" when referring to the Cuban government.

Miguelito shook his head. "No," he repeated, "I am considered a dissident. Quiet, but a dissident. I would not be allowed to travel."

When he asked, I told Miguelito that yes, I had traveled a great deal, leaving behind a turbulent New York childhood, abandoning opium dreams, dragons and mermaids. I told him, even though I could see his envy, that yes, freedom was tangible, once you had known it you could keep it with you, carry it inside, treasure it even if you had to keep it secret.

Now, as my cousin stepped to the window of the house he'd lived in since birth, under the watchful eye of my great-grandmother's portrait, I felt a great tenderness for him, for his wife and child, and for his mother with her mercifully fading memory.

Aurora rose from her rocking chair and began closing windows. She looked nervous, anxious. Miguelito
reached out to stop her hand. "Leave them open," he commanded. His mother looked up at him mournfully. Both
women retreated, disappearing down the dark hallway, taking the child with them, holding onto the walls as they
walked. Before vanishing into the hallway, Aurora turned to
me and whispered, "What will become of us?"

"I want to know about freedom, but I am a quiet dissident," Miguelito offered, watching me intently. He looked so
much like a cowboy in a Western movie that I expected him to
whip out a gun and start shooting out the windows, over the
fluttering skirts of the trees in the park, toward the black Cuban
storm clouds which had always reminded me of wild horses.

"Here," he said, "everything is hypocrisy. I have to
be very careful. I want to write songs. I want to sing. A simpler freedom than travel, simpler than having choices. But
here it is impossible. It is too dangerous. No one can write
unless they belong to the Writers Union. To belong to the

Writers Union you must be selected by the government. You must write what they want you to write. Painting is the same, and dance, and drama. Songwriting. Everything is controlled. You have heard the term totalitarianism, right? I know they tell you that about us over there. You've heard about communists acting like robots, doing what they're told to do, saying what they're told to say." He imitated the stiff, mechanical movements of a cartoon robot. "Well, it's true, it's all true. Everything you've ever heard about us, it's true. That's what it's like here, total power for one man, total. And I know you must wonder, so I'm telling you. Because if I was from over there, I would wonder. I would want you to tell me, I would expect you to confide.

"This," my cousin continued, "is a poem the children memorize in school, 'Fidel is always present . . . as if his boots had wings'."

The words of the poem would have been lovely if the subject had been God or the angels. I felt terribly saddened for my cousin who wanted to write songs but could not, would not, without endangering his family by crossing the line from quiet dissident to prohibited voice.

"He treats us," my cousin said, gazing upward toward the crumbling ceiling, choosing his words carefully, "like children. Every little thing is decided for us, what we will study, where we will work, where we will live, where we will go on vacation, what we will eat for dinner."

Miguelito extracted a booklet from his pocket and handed it to me, flipping the pages to show me a series of entries on small rectangles of lined paper. "This is the only way I have ever in my entire life obtained food," he said. "I am only a little older than the revolution. So you see, since I was a very small child, this is all I have ever known." He was looking out the window again, speaking in a loud voice. "I don't enjoy the career they chose for me. It is technical work, productive, it has value, but it's not what I want to do. I feel paralyzed, strangled."

My mind was racing with empathy and new perceptions. My cousin had said he didn't care if he went to the prison camps, but he also said he had to be careful for his family's sake. He said there was nothing left to lose, yet here he was living in a portion of his father's house with a wife, child and an aging mother who needed him. So perhaps he was referring to the intangibles he had already lost: honor, dignity and integrity, liberty, equality and fraternity, all the noble, poetic promises represented on the island's coat of arms.

"Come," my cousin commanded. To me he seemed to have plenty of honor and dignity as he led me down the dark hallway. Integrity too, because here he was speaking openly about forbidden topics. The presence of an outsider, a foreigner, seemed to have loosened a flood of words he had been restraining around Cubans. I knew about Neighborhood Committees for the Defense of the Revolution because I read my human rights bulletins faithfully and because Amparo and Juan had told me what it was like to be watched by the neighbors, to be turned in to the secret police for any little complaint or for unauthorized gatherings of more than seven people meeting in a house or for possession of more butter than your ration coupons entitled you to buy.

I hoped Miguelito would close the windows next time he wanted to confide his longing for simple freedoms such as traveling or composing new songs. If my presence was going to hurl open a floodgate of honesty, I wanted to make sure we weren't overheard by suspicious neighbors.

Halfway down the hall, Miguelito stopped and pointed out a framed photograph of my mother when she was young and pregnant. "So you see," my cousin said, "you've been here in Cuba all along, hanging on the wall, waiting to be born."

Then he led me into a room with small high windows and old mahogany furniture. Carvings on the wood depicted peacocks, angels, cherubs, roses, palm trees. I had the impression I was in the depths of a forest, surrounded by dancers, hearing drums and wailing lyrics, praise and lamentations.

My cousin took me by the elbow. I could hear his wife reading to their son in another room. I was frightened, not by my cousin, but by the shadowy forests of the room, haunted by music and ballerinas, torn by a flurry of wings and fangs. Graceful palms, pale dancers, hills, horses and cattle, vultures, parrots, all were here: as were sky, sun, pastures, fields of sugarcane.

"This," my cousin told me, still holding onto my elbow in a protective gesture, "is the room where my father killed himself just a few months ago."

I knew Miguel had died recently but I didn't know that his death had been a suicide. The battling of wings and fangs was intense now. The music was deafening. I wondered if Miguelito was aware of the angels and demons in this room, the ambushes, attacks, struggles, the singing and hissing.

Gradually, the feeling of being trapped passed, but the angels and demons still surrounded us. I could see some of the demons, and I could hear the singing of angels. The room was still dark and mysterious, still a wilderness of primitive jungle and savage farm. I was beginning to feel at home in this room. Everything was familiar, the visions, the music, the wind.

Miguelito drew me over to one side of the room, under a high window guarded by a large crucifix. "Right here," he said, "is where my father killed himself. I knew he was going to do it because he told me. He was old and sick, and he was discouraged. He knew he wasn't getting better, nothing was getting better, and something in his spirit was already dead. The suffering was too much for him. So he took a clean white cloth and wrapped it around his neck and tied it to the window, there, and strangled himself."

I remembered Miguel as a brilliant singer and dancer, a man who with his voice could bring to life mountains, islands, the sea. I remembered how triumphant Miguel had felt after the revolution was over, when truckloads of bearded troops were roaming Havana, cheered by jubilant crowds. During the summer of 1960, the songs of my great-uncle Miguel had been like float-ing balloons filled with hope, songs promising liberty and justice.

Miguelito now picked up a guitar with broken strings, and began to sing his father's words. Then he leaned the guitar against a wall, and continued speaking. "I came into this room and found him dead."

A wing bumped me, and I moved across the room, gazing into the walls, seeing scenes from Miguel's childhood on the farm which once belonged to his parents and later to Gabriel. I thought of the legendary Cuban troubadours who had risked their lives by walking the streets of Havana during the early 1930's, singing protest songs during a student rebellion against the hated dictator Machado.

Miguel had been one of those singers, and his songs had been an inspiration to the rebels, among them his brother Daniel, who had also moved to Havana as a young man, and was one of the university students leading the rebellion. I remembered how Miguel had once told me that Machado's secret police tried to shoot him down for singing in the streets. He had laughed, saying "But now here I am, doing the same for another revolution, against another tyrant, and now we've won, and no one can ever tell me to stop singing." But he'd been wrong. They had told him to stop.

Scattered throughout the haunted room, angels whispered and demons shrieked.

Miguelito was silent for a long moment. Then he startled me by asking, "And you, have you ever considered suicide?"

Yes, it was true, Miguelito and I were very much alike. I nodded. All around me, dancers twirled embraced by royal palms. The ghostly white legs of the dancers were luminescent, showered by moonlight. The trees accompanying them pirouetted. We were in the mountains, in a village hidden by jungle.

"Yes," I answered, "I did consider suicide, I considered it seriously." I was thinking of my youth in Spanish Harlem, of the opium dreams, the dragons and sirens.

"Aah," my cousin said, "you see." And somehow I felt certain that his response was one of recognition, an awareness of our similarity.

Miguelito closed his eyes. He was listening to the music around us. I began to realize that not all of the songs in this room were coming from angels or from my great-uncle's ghost. Miguelito was also singing, his voice flowing through the hot moist air, mingling with the humming of angels and clawing of demons.

When his song ended, my cousin opened his eyes abruptly.

"I have considered suicide myself," Miguelito said, "very profoundly."

The music resumed as his confession ended.

"Sometimes," Miguelito said, speaking above the melody and rhythm of his own imagination, "I talk to God. Sometimes I ask God to help me, but here I am, still waiting, feeling that I've been forgotten."

A cloud of striped butterflies came flickering across the room. I could see cobblestone streets, a belltower, caves, flying fish, all the experiences of my great-uncle Miguel's life, traveling through the room, trapped here, like small caged songbirds caught wild in the mountains and carried into town in bamboo cages, to be hung in quiet patios, and taken out for walks at sunset.

"Yes," Miguelito repeated, "I have considered suicide."

Maturin M. Ballou

CREOLE LADIES, MARTI THE SMUGGLER, BULLFIGHTING

WE HAVE SAID that the Creole ladies never stir abroad except in the national volante, and whatever their domestic habits may be, they are certainly, in this respect, good *housekeepers.* A Cuban belle could never, we fancy, be made to understand the pleasures of that most profitless of all employments, spinning street-yarn. While our ladies are busily engaged in sweeping the sidewalks of Chestnut-street and Broadway with their silk flounces, she wisely leaves that business to the gangs of criminals

Newspaperman Maturin M. Ballou (1820–1895), one of the founders of The Boston Globe, *visited Cuba for a year with his wife; his* History of Cuba *appeared shortly afterward.*

who perform the office with their limbs chained, and a ball attached to preserve their equilibrium. It is perhaps in part owing to these habits that the feet of the Cuban señorita are such a marvel of smallness and delicacy, seemingly made rather for ornament than for use. She knows the charm of the *petit pied bien chaussé* that delights the Parisian, and accordingly, as you catch a glimpse of it, as she steps into the volante, you perceive that it is daintily shod in a French slipper, the sole of which is scarcely more substantial in appearance than writing paper.[1]

The feet of the Havana ladies are made for ornament and for dancing. Though with a roundness of figure that leaves nothing to be desired in symmetry of form, yet they are light as a sylph, clad in muslin and lace, so languid and light that it would seem as if a breeze might waft them away like a summer cloud. They are passionately fond of dancing, and tax the endurance of the gentlemen in their heroic worship of Terpsichore. Inspired by the thrilling strains of those Cuban airs, which are at once so sweet and brilliant, they glide or whirl through the mazes of the dance hour after hour, until daylight breaks upon the scene of fairy revel. Then, "exhausted but not satiated," they betake themselves to sleep, to dream of the cadences of some Cuban Strauss, and to beat time in imagination to the lively notes, and to dream over the soft words and winning glances they have exchanged.

Beautiful as eastern houris, there is a striking and endearing charm about the Cuban ladies, their very motion being replete with a native grace; every limb elastic and supple. Their voices are sweet and low, "an excellent thing in woman," and the subdued tone of their complexions is relieved by the arch vivacity of night-black eyes that alternately swim in melting lustre or sparkle in expressive glances. Their costume is never ostentatious, though costly; the most delicate muslin, the finest linen, the richest silk, the most exquisitely made satin shoes,—these, of course, render their chaste attire exceedingly expensive. There are no "strong-minded" women among them, nor is it hardly possible to conceive of any extremity that could induce them to get up a woman's right convention—a suspension of fans and volantes might produce such a phenomenon, but we very much doubt it.

The Creole ladies lead a life of decided ease and pleasure. What little work they do is very light and lady-like, a little sewing or embroidery; the bath and the *siesta* divide the sultry hours of the day. They wait until nearly sun-set for the drive in the dear volante, and then go to respond by sweet smiles to the salutations of the *caballeros* on the Paseoes, and after the long twilight to the Plaza de Armas, to listen to the governor's military band, and then perhaps to join the mazy dance. Yet they are capable of deep and high feeling, and when there was a prospect of the liberation of the island, these fair patriots it will be remembered gave their most precious jewels and ornaments as a contribution to the glorious cause of liberty.

ONE OF THE most successful villains whose story will be written in history, is a man named Marti, as well known in Cuba as the person of the governor-general himself. Formerly he was notorious as a smuggler and half pirate on the coast of the island, being a daring and accomplished leader of reckless men. At one time he bore the title of King of the Isle of Pines, where was his principal rendezvous, and from whence he dispatched his vessels, small, fleet crafts, to operate in the neighboring waters.

His story, well known in Cuba and to the home government, bears intimately upon our subject.

When Tacon landed on the island, and became governor-general, he found the revenue laws in a sad condition, as well as the internal regulations of the island; and, with a spirit of mingled justice and oppression, he determined to do something in the way of reform.[2] The Spanish marine sent out to regulate the maritime matters of the island, lay idly in port, the officers passing their time on shore, or in giving balls and dances on the decks of their vessels. Tacon saw that one of the first moves for him to make was to suppress the smuggling upon the coast, at all hazards; and to this end he set himself directly to work. The maritime force at his command was at once detailed upon this service, and they coasted night and day, but without the least success against the smugglers. In vain were all the vigilance and activity of Tacon and his agents—they accomplished nothing.

At last, finding that all his expeditions against them failed, partly from the adroitness and bravery of the smugglers, and partly from the want of pilots among the shoals and rocks that they frequented, a large and tempting reward was offered to any one of them who would desert from his comrades and act in this capacity in behalf of the government. At the same time, a double sum, most princely in amount, was offered for the person of one Marti, dead or alive, who was known to be the leader of the lawless rovers who thus defied the government. These rewards were freely promulgated, and posted so as to reach the ears and eyes of those whom they concerned; but even these seemed to produce no effect, and the government officers were at a loss how to proceed in the matter.

It was a dark, cloudy night in Havana, some three or four months subsequent to the issuing of these placards announcing the rewards as referred to, when two sentinels were pacing backwards and forwards before the main entrance to the governor's palace, just opposite the grand plaza. A little before midnight, a man, wrapped in a cloak, was watching them from behind the statue of Ferdinand, near the fountain, and, after observing that the two soldiers acting as sentinels paced their brief walk so as to meet each other, and then turn their backs as they separated, leaving a brief moment in the interval when the eyes of both were turned away from the entrance they were placed to guard, seemed to calculate upon passing them unobserved. It was an exceedingly delicate manœuver, and required great care and dexterity to effect it; but, at last, it was adroitly done, and the stranger sprang lightly through the entrance, secreting himself behind one of the pillars in the inner court of the palace. The sentinels paced on undisturbed.

The figure which had thus stealthily effected an entrance, now sought the broad stairs that led to the governor's suit of apartments, with a confidence that evinced a perfect knowledge of the place. A second guard-post was to be passed at the head of the stairs; but, assuming an air of authority, the stranger offered a cold military salute and pressed forward, as though there was not the most distant question of his right so to do; and thus avoiding all suspicion in the guard's mind, he boldly entered the governor's reception room unchallenged, and closed the door behind him. In a large easy chair sat the commander-in-chief, busily engaged in writing, but alone. An expression of undisguised satisfaction passed across the weather-beaten countenance of the new comer at this state of affairs, as he coolly cast off his cloak and tossed it over his arm, and then proceeded to wipe the perspiration from his face. The governor, looking up with surprise, fixed his keen eyes upon the intruder,—

"Who enters here, unannounced, at this hour?" he asked, sternly, while he regarded the stranger earnestly.

"One who has information of value for the governor-general. You are Tacon, I suppose?"

"I am. What would you with me? or, rather, how did you pass my guard unchallenged?"

"Of that anon. Excellency, you have offered a handsome reward for information concerning the rovers of the gulf?"

"Ha! yes. What of them?" said Tacon, with undisguised interest.

"Excellency, I must speak with caution," continued the new comer; "otherwise I may condemn and sacrifice myself."

"You have naught to fear on that head. The offer of reward for evidence against the scapegraces also vouchsafes a pardon to the informant. You may speak on, without fear for yourself, even though you may be one of the very confederation itself."

"You offer a reward, also, in addition, for the discovery of Marti,—Captain Marti, of the smugglers—do you not?"

"We do, and will gladly make good the promise of reward for any and all information upon the subject," replied Tacon.

"First, Excellency, do you give me your knightly word

that you will grant a free pardon to *me*, if I reveal all that you require to know, even embracing the most secret hiding-places of the rovers?"

"I pledge you my word of honor," said the commander.

"No matter how heinous in the sight of the law my offences may have been, still you will pardon me, under the king's seal?"

"I will, if you reveal truly and to any good purpose," answered Tacon, weighing in his mind the purpose of all this precaution.

"Even if I were a leader among the rovers, myself?"

The governor hesitated for a moment, canvassing in a single glance the subject before him, and then said:

"Even then, be you whom you may; if you are able and will honestly pilot our ships and reveal the secrets of Marti and his followers, you shall be rewarded as our proffer sets forth, and yourself receive a free pardon."

"Excellency, I think I know your character well enough to trust you, else I should not have ventured here."

"Speak then; my time is precious," was the impatient reply of Tacon.

"Then, Excellency, the man for whom you have offered the largest reward, dead or alive, is now before you!"

"And you are——"

"Marti!"

The governor-general drew back in astonishment, and cast his eyes towards a brace of pistols that lay within reach of his right hand; but it was only for a single moment, when he again assumed entire self-control, and said,

"I shall keep my promise, sir, provided you are faithful, though the laws call loudly for your punishment, and even now you are in my power. To insure your faithfulness, you must remain at present under guard." Saying which, he rang a silver bell by his side, and issued a verbal order to the attendant who answered it. Immediately after, the officer of the watch entered, and Marti was placed in confinement, with orders to render him comfortable until he was sent for. His name remained a secret with the commander; and thus the night scene closed.

On the following day, one of the men-of-war that lay idly beneath the guns of Moro Castle suddenly became the scene of utmost activity, and, before noon, had weighed her anchor, and was standing out into the gulf stream. Marti, the smuggler, was on board, as her pilot; and faithfully did he guide the ship, on the discharge of his treacherous business, among the shoals and bays of the coast for nearly a month, revealing every secret haunt of the rovers, exposing their most valuable depots and well-selected rendezvous; and many a smuggling craft was taken and destroyed. The amount of money and property thus secured was very great; and Marti returned with the ship to claim his reward from the governor-general, who, well satisfied with the manner in which the rascal had fulfilled his agreement, and betrayed those comrades who were too faithful to be tempted to treachery themselves, summoned Marti before him.

"As you have faithfully performed your part of our agreement," said the governor-general, "I am now prepared to comply with the articles on my part. In this package you will find a free and unconditional pardon for all your past offenses against the laws. And here is an order on the treasury for—"

"Excellency, excuse me. The pardon I gladly receive. As to the sum of money you propose to give me, let me make you a proposition. Retain the money; and, in place of it, guarantee to me the right to fish in the neighborhood of the city, and declare the trade in fish contraband to all except my agents. This will richly repay me, and I will erect a public market of stone at my own expense, which shall be an ornament to the city, and which at the expiration of a specified number of years shall revert to the government, with all right and title to the fishery.

Tacon was pleased at the idea of a superb fish-market, which should eventually revert to the government, and also at the idea of saving the large sum of money covered by the promised reward. The singular proposition of the smuggler was duly considered and acceded to, and Marti was declared in legal form to possess for the future sole right to fish in the neighborhood of the city, or to sell the article in any form, and he at once assumed the rights that the order guaranteed to him. Having in his roving life learned all the best fishing-grounds, he furnished the city bountifully with the article, and reaped yearly an immense profit, until, at the close of the period for which the monopoly was granted, he was the richest man on the island. According to the agreement, the fine market and its privilege reverted to the government at the time specified, and the monopoly has ever since been rigorously enforced.

Marti, now possessed of immense wealth, looked about him, to see in what way he could most profitably invest it to insure a handsome and sure return. The idea struck him if he could obtain the monopoly of theatricals in Havana on some such conditions as he had done that of the right to fish off its shores, he could still further increase his ill-gotten wealth. He obtained the monopoly, on condition that he should erect one of the largest and finest theatres in the world, which he did, as herein described, locating the same just outside the city walls. With the conditions of the monopoly, the writer is not conversant.

Many romantic stories are told of Marti; but the one we have here related is the only one that is authenticated, and which has any bearing upon the present work.

OF ALL THE games and sports of the Cubans, that of the bull-fight is the most cruel and fearful, and without one redeeming feature in its indulgence. The arena for the exhibitions in the neighborhood of Havana is just across the harbor at Regla, a small town, having a most worn and dilapidated appearance.[3] This place was formerly the haunt of pirates, upon whose depredations and boldness the government, for reasons best known to itself, shut its official eyes; more latterly it has been the hailing place for slavers, whose crafts have not yet entirely disappeared, though the rigor of the English and French cruisers in the Gulf has rendered it necessary for them to seek a less exposed rendezvous. Of the Spanish marine they entertain no fear; there is the most perfect understanding on this point, treaty stipulations touching the slave-trade, between Spain, England and France, to the contrary notwithstanding.[4] But we were referring to the subject of the bull-fights. The arena at Regla, for this purpose, is a large circular enclosure of sufficient dimensions to seat six thousand people, and affording perhaps a little more than half an acre of ground for the fight.

The seats are raised one above another in a circle around, at a secure height from the dangerous struggle which is sure to characterize each exhibition. On the occasion when the writer was present, after a flourish of trumpets, a large bull was let loose from a stall opening into the pit of the enclosure, where three Spaniards (*toreadors*), one on foot and two on horseback, were ready to receive him, the former armed with a sword, the latter with spears. They were three hardened villains, if the human countenance can be relied upon as shadowing forth the inner man, seemingly reckless to the last degree, but very expert, agile, and wary. These men commenced at once to worry and torment the bull until they should arouse him to a state of frenzy. Short spears were thrust into his neck and sides with rockets attached, which exploded into his very flesh, burning and affrighting the poor creature. Thrusts from the horsemen's spears were made into his flesh, and while he was bleeding thus at every pore, gaudy colors were shaken before his glowing eyes; and wherever he turned to escape his tormentors, he was sure to be met with some freshly devised expedient of torment, until at last the creature became indeed perfectly infuriated and frantically mad. Now the fight was in earnest!

In vain did the bull plunge gallantly and desperately at his enemies, they were far too expert for him. They had made this game their business perhaps for years. Each rush he made upon them was easily avoided, and he passed them by, until, in his headlong course, he thrust his horns deep into the boards of the enclosure. The idea, of course, was not to give him any fatal wounds at the outset, and thus dispatch him at once, but to worry and torment him to the last. One of the gladiators now attacked him closely with the sword, and dexterously wounded him in the back of the neck at each plunge the animal made towards him, at the same time springing on one side to avoid the shock. After a long fight and a grand flourish of trumpets, the most skilful of the swordsmen stood firm and received the infuriated beast on the point of his weapon, which was aimed at a fatal spot above the frontlet, leading direct to the brain. The effect was electrical, and like dropping a curtain upon a play: the animal staggered, reeled a moment, and fell dead! Three bulls were thus destroyed, the last one in his frenzy goring a fine spirited horse, on which one of the gladiators was mounted, to death, and trampling his rider fearfully. During the exhibition, the parties in the arena were encouraged to feats of daring by the waving of handkerchiefs and scarfs in the hands of the fair señoras and señoritas. Indeed there is generally a young girl trained to the business, who takes a part in the arena with the matadors against the bull. The one thus engaged, on the occasion here referred to, could not have exceeded seventeen years in age.

1 "Her hands and feet are as small and delicate as those of a child. She wears the finest satin slippers, with scarcely any soles, which, luckily, are never destined to touch the street." —*Countess Merlin's Letters.*

2 Tacon governed Cuba four years, from 1834 to 1838.

3 Regla now contains some seven thousand inhabitants, and is chiefly engaged in the exportation of molasses, which is here kept in large tanks.

4 An intelligent letter-writer estimates the present annual importation of slaves at not less than 10,000 souls, direct from Africa.

Wallace Stevens

ACADEMIC DISCOURSE AT HAVANA

I

CANARIES IN THE morning, orchestras
In the afternoon, balloons at night. That is
A difference, at least, from nightingales,
Jehovah and the great sea-worm. The air
Is not so elemental nor the earth
So near.

       But the sustenance of the wilderness
Does not sustain us in the metropoles.

Despite his wide recognition as one of America's foremost poets, Wallace Stevens (1879–1955) never quit his day job as vice president of an insurance company. He visited Havana in 1923; "Academic Discourse at Havana" appeared the following year.

II

Life is an old casino in a park.

The bills of the swans are flat upon the ground.

A most desolate wind has chilled Rouge-Fatima

And a grand decadence settles down like cold.

III

The swans . . . Before the bills of the swans fell flat

Upon the ground, and before the chronicle

Of affected homage foxed so many books,

They warded the blank waters of the lakes

And island canopies which were entailed

To that casino. Long before the rain

Swept through its boarded windows and the leaves

Filled its encrusted fountains, they arrayed

The twilights of the mythy goober khan.

The centuries of excellence to be

Rose out of promise and became the sooth

  Of trombones floating in the trees.

The toil
Of thought evoked a peace eccentric to
The eye and tinkling to the ear. Gruff drums
Could beat, yet not alarm the populace.
The indolent progressions of the swans
Made earth come right; a peanut parody
For peanut people.

And serener myth
Conceiving from its perfect plenitude,
Lusty as June, more fruitful than the weeks
Of ripest summer, always lingering
To touch again the hottest bloom, to strike
Once more the longest resonance, to cap
The clearest woman with apt weed, to mount
The thickest man on thickest stallion-back,
This urgent, competent, serener myth
Passed like a circus.

Politic man ordained
Imagination as the fateful sin.
Grandmother and her basketful of pears
Must be the crux for our compendia.
That's world enough, and more, if one includes
Her daughters to the peached and ivory wench
For whom the towers are built. The burgher's
    breast,
And not a delicate ether star-impaled,
Must be the place for prodigy, unless
Prodigious things are tricks. The world is not
The bauble of the sleepless nor a word
That should import a universal pith
To Cuba. Jot these milky matters down.
They nourish Jupiters. Their casual pap
Will drop like sweetness in the empty nights
When too great rhapsody is left annulled
And liquorish prayer provokes new sweats; so, so:
Life is an old casino in a wood.

IV

Is the function of the poet here mere sound,

Subtler than the ornatest prophecy,

To stuff the ear? It causes him to make

His infinite repetition and alloys

Of pick of ebon, pick of halcyon.

It weighs him with nice logic for the prim.

As part of nature he is part of us.

His rarities are ours: may they be fit

And reconcile us to our selves in those

True reconcilings, dark, pacific words,

And the adroiter harmonies of their fall.

Close the cantina. Hood the chandelier.

The moonlight is not yellow but a white

That silences the ever-faithful town.

How pale and how possessed a night it is,

How full of exhalations of the sea . . .

All this is older than its oldest hymn,

Has no more meaning than tomorrow's bread.

But let the poet on his balcony
Speak and the sleepers in their sleep shall move,
Waken, and watch the moonlight on their floors.
This may be benediction, sepulcher,
And epitaph. It may, however, be
An incantation that the moon defines
By mere example opulently clear.
And the old casino likewise may define
An infinite incantation of our selves
In the grand decadence of the perished swans.

William Cullen Bryant

HAVANA LETTER

Havana, April 10, 1849.

I FIND THAT it requires a greater effort of resolution to sit down to the writing of a long letter in this soft climate, than in the country I have left. I feel a temptation to sit idly, and let the grateful wind from the sea, coming in at the broad windows, flow around me, or read, or talk, as I happen

---

William Cullen Bryant (1794–1878) abandoned a law career for magazine journalism, eventually landing the position of editor of the New York Evening Post. *He published his travel observations in the* Post *and later collected them in* Letters of a Traveller.

to have a book or a companion. That there is something in a tropical climate which indisposes one to vigorous exertion I can well believe, from what I experience in myself, and what I see around me. The ladies do not seem to take the least exercise, except an occasional drive on the Paseo, or public park; they never walk out, and when they are shopping, which is no less the vocation of their sex here than in other civilized countries, they never descend from their *volantes,* but the goods are brought out by the obsequious shopkeeper, and the lady makes her choice and discusses the price as she sits in her carriage.

Yet the women of Cuba show no tokens of delicate health. Freshness of color does not belong to a latitude so near the equator, but they have plump figures, placid, unwrinkled countenances, a well-developed bust, and eyes, the brilliant languor of which is not the languor of illness. The girls as well as the young men, have rather narrow shoulders, but as they advance in life, the chest, in the women particularly, seems to expand from year to year, till it attains an amplitude by no means common in our country. I fully believe that this effect, and their general health, in spite of the inaction in which they pass their lives, is owing to the free circulation of air through their apartments.

For in Cuba, the women as well as the men may be said to live in the open air. They know nothing of close rooms, in all the island, and nothing of foul air, and to this, I have no doubt, quite as much as to the mildness of the temperature, the friendly effect of its climate upon invalids from the north is to be ascribed. Their ceilings are extremely lofty, and the wide windows, extending from the top of the room to the floor and guarded by long perpendicular bars of iron, are without glass, and when closed are generally only closed with blinds which, while they break the force of the wind when it is too strong, do not exclude the air. Since I have been on the island, I may be said to have breakfasted and dined and supped and slept in the open air, in an atmosphere which is never in repose except for a short time in the morning after sunrise. At other times a breeze is always stirring, in the day-time bringing in the air from the ocean, and at night drawing it out again to the sea.

In walking through the streets of the towns in Cuba, I have been entertained by the glimpses I had through the ample windows, of what was going on in the parlors. Sometimes a curtain hanging before them allowed me only a sight of the small hands which clasped the bars of the grate, and the dusky faces and dark eyes peeping into the street and scanning the passers by. At other times, the whole room was seen, with its furniture, and its female forms sitting in languid postures, courting the breeze as it entered from without. In the evening, as I passed along the narrow sidewalk of the narrow streets, I have been startled at finding myself almost in the midst of a merry party gathered about the window of a brilliantly lighted room, and chattering the soft Spanish of the island in voices that sounded strangely near to me. I have spoken of their languid postures: they love to recline on sofas; their houses are filled with rocking-chairs imported from the United States; they are fond of sitting in chairs tilted against the wall, as we sometimes do at home. Indeed they go beyond us in this respect; for in Cuba they have invented a kind of chair which, by lowering the back and raising the knees, places the sitter precisely in the posture he would take if he sat in a chair leaning backward against a wall. It is a luxurious attitude, I must own, and I do not wonder that it is a favorite with lazy people, for it relieves one of all the trouble of keeping the body upright.

It is the women who form the large majority of the worshippers in the churches. I landed here in Passion Week, and the next day was Holy Thursday, when not a vehicle on wheels of any sort is allowed to be seen in the streets; and the ladies, contrary to their custom during the rest of the year, are obliged to resort to the churches on foot. Negro servants of both sexes were seen passing to and fro, carrying mats on which their mistresses were to kneel in the morning service. All the white female population, young and old, were dressed in black, with black lace veils. In the afternoon, three wooden or waxen images of the size of life, representing Christ in the different stages of his passion, were placed in the spacious Church of St. Catharine, which was so thronged that I found it difficult to enter. Near the door was a figure of the Saviour sinking under the weight of his cross, and the worshippers were kneeling to kiss his feet. Aged negro men and women, half-naked negro children, ladies richly attired, little girls in Parisian dresses, with lustrous black eyes and a profusion of ringlets, cast themselves down before the image, and pressed their lips to its feet in a passion of devotion. Mothers led up their little ones, and showed them how to perform this act of adoration. I saw matrons and young women rise from it with their eyes red with tears.

The next day, which was Good Friday, about twilight, a long procession came trailing slowly through the streets under my window, bearing an image of the dead Christ, lying upon a cloth of gold. It was accompanied by a body of soldiery, holding their muskets reversed, and a band playing plaintive tunes; the crowd uncovered their heads as it passed. On Saturday morning, at ten o'clock, the solemnities of holy week were over; the bells rang a merry peal; hundreds of volantes and drays which had stood ready harnessed, rushed into the streets; the city became suddenly noisy with the rattle of wheels and the tramp of horses; the shops which had been shut for the last two days, were opened; and the ladies, in white or light-colored muslins, were proceeding in their volantes to purchase at the shops their costumes for the Easter festivities.

I passed the evening on the *Plaza de Armas,* a public square in front of the Governor's house, planted with palms and other trees, paved with broad flags, and bordered with a row of benches. It was crowded with people in their best dresses, the ladies mostly in white, and without bonnets, for the bonnet in this country is only worn while travelling. Chairs had been placed for them in a double row around the edge of the square, and a row of volantes surrounded the square, in each of which sat two or more ladies, the ample folds of their muslin dresses flowing out on each side over the steps of the carriage. The Governor's band played various airs, martial and civic, with great beauty of execution. The music continued for two hours, and the throng, with only occasional intervals of conversation, seemed to give themselves up wholly to the enjoyment of listening to it.

It was a bright moonlight night, so bright that one might almost see to read, and the temperature the finest I can conceive, a gentle breeze rustling among the palms overhead. I was surprised at seeing around me so many fair brows and snowy necks. It is the moonlight, said I to myself, or perhaps it is the effect of the white dresses, for the complexions of these ladies seem to differ several shades from those which I saw yesterday at the churches. A female acquaintance has since given me another solution of the matter.

"The reason," she said, "of the difference you perceived is this, that during the ceremonies of holy week they take off the *cascarilla* from their faces, and appear in their natural complexions."

I asked the meaning of the word *cascarilla*, which I did not remember to have heard before.

"It is the favorite cosmetic of the island, and is made of egg-shells finely pulverized. They often fairly plaster their faces with it. I have seen a dark-skinned lady as white almost as marble at a ball. They will sometimes, at a morning call or an evening party, withdraw to repair the *cascarilla* on their faces."

I do not vouch for this tale, but tell it "as it was told to me." Perhaps, after all, it was the moonlight which had produced this transformation, though I had noticed something of the same improvement of complexion just before sunset, on the Paseo Isabel, a public park without the city walls, planted with rows of trees, where, every afternoon, the gentry of Havana drive backward and forward in their volantes, with each a glittering harness, and a liveried negro bestriding, in large jack-boots, the single horse which draws the vehicle.

I had also the same afternoon visited the receptacle into which the population of the city are swept when the game of life is played out—the Camp Santo, as it is called, or public cemetery of Havana. Going out of the city at the gate nearest the sea, I passed through a street of the wretchedest houses I had seen; the ocean was roaring at my right on the coral rocks which form the coast. The dingy habitations were soon left behind, and I saw the waves, pushed forward by a fresh wind, flinging their spray almost into the road; I next entered a short avenue of trees, and in a few minutes the volante stopped at the gate of the cemetery. In a little inclosure before the entrance, a few starveling flowers of Europe were cultivated, but the wild plants of the country flourished luxuriantly on the rich soil within. A thick wall surrounded the cemetery, in which were rows of openings for coffins, one above the other, where the more opulent of the dead were entombed. The coffin is thrust in endwise, and the opening closed with a marble slab bearing an inscription.

Most of these niches were already occupied, but in the earth below, by far the greater part of those who die at Havana, are buried without a monument or a grave which they are allowed to hold a longer time than is necessary for their bodies to be consumed in the quicklime which is thrown upon them. Every day fresh trenches are dug into which their bodies are thrown, generally without coffins. Two of these, one near each wall of the cemetery, were waiting for the funerals. I saw where the spade had divided the bones of those who were buried there last, and thrown up the broken fragments, mingled with masses of lime, locks of hair, and bits of clothing. Without the walls was a receptacle in which the skulls and other larger bones, dark with the mould of the grave, were heaped.

Two or three persons were walking about the cemetery when we first entered, but it was now at length the cool of the day, and the funerals began to arrive. They brought in first a rude black coffin, broadest at the extremity which contained the head, and placing it at the end of one of the trenches, hurriedly produced a hammer and nails to fasten the lid before letting it down, when it was found that the box was too shallow at the narrower extremity. The lid was removed for a moment and showed the figure of an old man in a threadbare black coat, white pantaloons, and boots. The negroes who bore it beat out the bottom with the hammer, so as to allow the lid to be fastened over the feet. It was then nailed down firmly with coarse

nails, the coffin was swung into the trench, and the earth shovelled upon it. A middle-aged man, who seemed to be some relative of the dead, led up a little boy close to the grave and
watched the process of filling it. They spoke to each other and
smiled, stood till the pit was filled to the surface, and the bear-
ers had departed, and then retired in their turn. This was one
of the more respectable class of funerals. Commonly the dead
are piled without coffins, one above the other, in the trenches.

The funerals now multiplied. The corpse of a little
child was brought in, uncoffined; and another, a young man
who, I was told, had cut his throat for love, was borne towards
one of the niches in the wall. I heard loud voices, which seemed
to proceed from the eastern side of the cemetery, and which, I
thought at first, might be the recitation of a funeral service; but
no funeral service is said at these graves; and after a time, I perceived that they came from the windows of a long building
which overlooked one side of the burial ground. It was a mad-
house. The inmates, exasperated at the spectacle before them,
were gesticulating from the windows—the women screaming

and the men shouting, but no attention was paid to their uproar. A lady, however, a stranger to the island, who visited the Campo Santo that afternoon, was so affected by the sights and sounds of the place, that she was borne out weeping and almost in convulsions. As we left the place, we found a crowd of volantes about the gate; a pompous bier, with rich black hangings, drew up; a little beyond, we met one of another kind—a long box, with glass sides and ends, in which lay the corpse of a woman, dressed in white, with a black veil thrown over the face.

The next day the festivities, which were to indemnify the people for the austerities of Lent and of Passion Week, began. The cock-pits were opened during the day, and masked balls were given in the evening at the theatres. You know, probably, that cock-fighting is the principal diversion of the island, having entirely supplanted the national spectacle of bull-baiting. Cuba, in fact, seemed to me a great poultry-yard. I heard the crowing of cocks in all quarters, for the game-cock is the noisiest and most beautiful of birds, and is perpetually uttering his notes of defiance. In the villages I saw the veterans of the pit, a strong-legged race, with their combs cropped smooth to the head, the feathers plucked from every part of the body except their wings, and the tail docked like that of a coach horse, picking up their food in the lanes among the chickens. One old cripple I remember to have seen in the little town of Guines, stiff with wounds received in combat, who had probably got a furlough for life, and who, while limping among his female companions, maintained a sort of strut in his gait, and now and then stopped to crow defiance to the world. The peasants breed game-cocks and bring them to market; amateurs in the town train them for their private amusement. Dealers in game-cocks are as common as horse-jockies with us, and every village has its cock-pit.

I went on Monday to the *Valla de Gallos,* situated in that part of Havana which lies without walls. Here, in a spacious inclosure, were two amphitheatres of benches, roofed, but without walls, with a circular area in the midst. Each was crowded with people, who were looking at a cockfight, and half of whom seemed vociferating with all their might. I mounted one of the outer benches, and saw one of the birds laid dead by the other in a few minutes. Then was heard the chink of gold and silver pieces, as the betters stepped into the area and paid their wagers; the slain bird was carried out and thrown on the ground, and the victor, taken into the hands of his owner, crowed loudly in celebration of his victory. Two other birds were brought in, and the cries of those who offered wagers were heard on all sides. They ceased at last, and the cocks were put down to begin the combat. They fought warily at first, but at length began to strike in earnest, the blood flowed, and the bystanders were heard to vociferate, *"ahí están peleando"**—*"mata! mata! mata!"*† gesticulating at the same time with great violence, and new wagers were laid as the interest of the combat increased. In ten minutes one of the birds was dispatched, for the combat never ends till one of them has his death-wound.

In the mean time several other combats had begun in smaller pits, which lay within the same inclosure, but were not surrounded with circles of benches. I looked upon the throng engaged in this brutal sport, with eager gestures and loud cries, and could not help thinking how soon this noisy crowd would lie in heaps in the pits of the Campo Santo.

In the evening was a masked ball in the Tacon Theatre, a spacious building, one of the largest of its kind in the world. The pit, floored over, with the whole depth of the stage open to the back wall of the edifice, furnished a ballroom of immense size. People in grotesque masks, in hoods or fancy dresses, were mingled with a throng clad in the ordinary costume, and Spanish dances were performed to the music of a numerous band. A well-dressed crowd filled the first and second tier of boxes. The Creole smokes everywhere, and seemed astonished when the soldier who stood at the door ordered him to throw away his lighted segar before entering. Once upon the floor, however, he lighted another segar in defiance of the prohibition.

The Spanish dances, with their graceful movements, resembling the undulations of the sea in its gentlest moods, are nowhere more gracefully performed than in Cuba, by the young women born on the island. I could not help thinking, however, as I looked on that gay crowd, on the quaint maskers, and the dancers whose flexible limbs seemed swayed to and fro by the breath of the music, that all this was soon to end at the Campo Santo, and I asked myself how many of all this crowd would be huddled uncoffined, when their sports were over, into the foul trenches of the public cemetery.

---

* "Now they are fighting!"

† "Kill! kill! kill!"

Acknowledgments

"Cuba Revisited" from *The View from the Ground* by Martha Gellhorn ©1988 by Martha Gellhorn. Reprinted by permission of Grove/Atlantic, Inc.

Excerpt from *Dreaming in Cuban* by Cristina Garcia ©1992 by Cristina Garcia. Reprinted by permission of Alfred A. Knopf, Inc..

Excerpt from *Havana Mañana* by Consuelo Hermer and Marjorie May ©1941 by Consuelo Hermer and Marjorie May. Reprinted by permission of Marjorie May.

"Cuban Childhood" from *Fidel and Religion* by Frei Betto ©1987 by Frei Betto. Reprinted by permission of Simon & Schuster.

Excerpt from *The Godfather Part II* ©1995 by Paramount Pictures. All rights reserved. Reprinted with permission of Paramount Pictures and Bertram Fields.

Excerpt from *Our Man in Havana* by Graham Greene ©1958 by William Heinemann Ltd. Reprinted by permission of Viking Penguin, a division of Penguin Books USA.

Excerpt from *The Book of Embraces* by Eduardo Galeano, translated from the Spanish by Cedric Belfrage with Mark Schafer, with the permission of W.W. Norton & Company, Inc. ©1989 by Eduardo Galeano. Reprinted by permission of W. W. Norton.

"Marlin off the Morro: A Cuban Letter" from *By-Line: Ernest Hemingway*, edited by William White ©1933 by Ernest Hemingway. Copyright renewed ©1961 by Mary Hemingway. Originally published in *Esquire* Magazine. Reprinted by permission of Scribner, an imprint of Simon & Schuster, Inc.

Excerpt from *Singing to Cuba* by Margarita Engle ©1993 by Arte Público Press. Reprinted by permission of Arte Público Press, University of Houston.

History of Cuba: or, Notes of a Traveller in the Tropics by Maturin M. Ballou is reproduced from original editions from the Bancroft Library and republished with their courtesy.

Excerpt from *Collected Poems* by Wallace Stevens ©1936 by Wallace Stevens and renewed 1964 by Holly Stevens. Reprinted by permission of Alfred A. Knopf, Inc.